Merry Christmas, Darling

Denise Devine

It's a pur-r-r-fect read!

Denise Devine

Merry Christmas, Darling

Counting Your Blessings Series, Book 1

Copyright 2014 by Denise Devine

www.deniseannettedevine.com

ISBN: 978-0-9915956-0-0

Beta Readers: Lori Ness and LuAnn Nies

Cover art by Christopher Edmund

Printed by CreateSpace, an Amazon.com Company

Available on Kindle and other retail outlets

To Kimberly Jo

Chapter 1

Friday evening, December 18

"Merry Christmas, darlin'."

Rock Henderson lounged against the doorway of Kimberly Jo Stratton's condominium, wearing a killer grin, a bright red Santa hat and a sleek tuxedo. One hand gripped a bottle of champagne; the other displayed two crystal flutes dangling upside-down between his long, slim fingers.

"I've brought you a little gift." He raised the bottle. "Vintage holiday cheer."

The grandfather clock in the opposite corner of her dining room chimed nine times as Kim tightened the sash around her pink chenille bathrobe. Rock's assistant had called at the last minute and said he would meet with her at four o'clock to discuss the war brewing between the residents of their condominium complex, but he never showed. By seven o'clock, she'd given up on him and changed into her pajamas and robe. How dare he drop by at this late hour, unapologetic, unconcerned about the situation and ready to party?

At her feet, a fawn Chihuahua with a white face yapped non-stop, jumping at her ankle like a wind-up toy. "Hush, Sasha," she snapped at the small dog, worried that all the commotion would draw attention and expose her plan to other tenants on her floor.

"You're five hours late, Henderson." She grabbed him by the lapels and hauled him into her living room. "Did you get lost?" Her gaze swept pointedly over his formal attire as she quickly shut the door.

"Or were you sidetracked by someone more glamorous than your lowly, working-class neighbor in 601E?"

Sasha looked up at Rock, let out a high-pitched yelp and dashed out of sight, her smooth tail curled between her legs.

He moved close, murmuring in Kim's ear. "I had an emergency, but I'm here now."

Rock Henderson, self-made millionaire and CEO of his own software design company, possessed the charm of a Hollywood heartthrob and the reputation of a ladies man who switched girlfriends as often as he changed the oil in his sports car.

"Come on, darlin'," he coaxed in that deep, throaty purr she'd heard him use on other women in the building, "just hear me out before you chew me out."

An emergency that required a tux? Yeah, right. A laughable excuse if she'd ever heard one. No way could she count on his cooperation if she couldn't even trust him to keep his word. He held out the bottle to show her the label, but she ignored his ill-timed bribe for standing her up, instead glaring into his chocolate, deep-set eyes. "You're drunk, Rock. Get on your private elevator and go home. And stop calling me darlin'!"

"I'm stone sober," Rock muttered as he strode past her, giving her a wry, sideways glance. "And for the record, I did not pass up our meeting for a hot date. I've just spent a long and difficult day dealing with an issue that literally landed on my doorstep."

He scanned her newly refurbished living room, illuminated only by the TV screen and twinkle lights on her Christmas tree. "Nice place you've got here," he said, abruptly changing the subject. He collapsed his broad, six-foot frame onto a cream loveseat, stretched out his legs and toed off his patent leather dress shoes. "Ah-h-h...feels good."

Kim followed him, ignoring the obvious compliment to flatter her into a good mood. They both knew her one-bedroom unit looked like

2

a walk-in closet compared to the ballroom-sized penthouse he occupied on the twentieth floor. She folded her arms and stared down at him. "Look, Rock, if all you want is someone to drink with—"

"Hey, hey, wait a minute." His dark brows arched as he set the champagne and flutes on the metal and glass coffee table. "You're the one who pressed my assistant repeatedly for this meeting. I'm simply providing refreshments." He pulled off his Santa hat and tossed it across the armrest of the loveseat. A thick lock of tousled black hair fell across his forehead. "What exactly do *you* want?"

Realizing she might actually have a chance to persuade him to accept her point of view, Kim sat on the opposite loveseat, picked up the TV remote and muted the sound of *Pillow Talk*. "I'd like to discuss what happened at the association meeting last week."

"Lucky me," he countered in a bored voice as he began peeling away the foil on the top of the bottle. "I've made it a rule to avoid those things. Most of the discussion is nothing but a complaint session. I have a corporation to run, clients to satisfy. It's immaterial to me whose overnight guests are taking up too many parking spots or whether we plant red flowers or gold ones along the front of the building."

If only...

The meeting last Wednesday nearly turned into an instant replay of a Jerry Springer episode, almost degrading to the point of chair throwing and a down-and-dirty brawl. Kim pushed the image of the emotionally charged crowd to the back of her mind as she edged closer to the coffee table separating her and Rock. "But you do understand the real issue in the latest controversy, don't you?"

He crumbled the foil into a ball and slipped it into his jacket pocket. "With all the arguing going on everywhere I turn, I'd have to be an alien from Mars to be ignorant of this one."

"Then tell me, which side are you on?" Her heart skipped a beat.

She hoped he understood how much was riding on his opinion. How drastically things could change if he elected to support the opposing view. "Are you for or against changing the bylaws to prohibit pets in this building?"

"Don't care either way." He unwound the wire cage protecting the cork then pointed the bottle toward the ceiling. "Pardon the pun, dar—my dear, but I don't have a dog in this fight." His brows drew together in concentration as he gripped the cork between his thumb and fingers and gently pulled. It made a long, low hiss as pressure escaped. After a few moments, he eased the cork out, but no bubbly liquid gushed forth. Only a slight mist curled above the opening.

"Rock, the preliminary vote ended in a tie and no one will budge." She leaned forward, placing her palms on the table. "Your vote could swing the decision either way."

At a time when she expected him to be serious, he chose to grin. "What you're really saying is that you want me to cast my vote in favor of the status quo so you can keep your mutt, right?"

A low growl unfurled under the Christmas tree followed by a succession of rapid snorts.

Rock glanced around in surprise. "What was *that*?"

"My dog and she isn't a mutt," Kim replied as Sasha glared at them from between two presents wrapped in red foil. "Here, Sasha." She patted the empty cushion next to her and smacked her lips. "Come on, sweetie. Rock's not going to hurt you."

The pint-sized canine crept from the shadows with pointed, white-tipped ears laid back, her bulbous brown eyes focused on Rock as she cautiously approached the loveseat. A ridge of fawn hair spiked in protest along her spine. Multi-colored lights twinkling on the tree reflected a rainbow of hues against her white chest and finger-length legs. She jumped on the loveseat and settled on Kim's lap with a snort, never taking her attention off the stranger sitting across from them.

"So that's what all the fuss is about, huh? No offense, but it looks like a fat rat." Grinning, Rock handed Kim a flute of champagne. His fingers grazed hers as the crystal changed hands. A sharp tingle sparked like a live wire up her arm and down her spine. Rock had that effect on women. All women, to be precise; but then, who could resist a tall, dark, handsome man who owned a penthouse on the Minneapolis riverfront and drove a red Jaguar?

She could and she'd made up her mind a long time ago that she always would. Growing up, she'd watched her mother fall in and out of love with men like him—successful, high rollers who loved the chase, but didn't know the meaning of commitment. The late Veronica Stratton would have schemed night and day to net a fish like Rock Henderson. Based upon her mother's experience, Kim knew first hand that you didn't catch a shark. The shark caught you and always left you deeply wounded in the water. She'd rather swim alone than take that chance.

Sasha glanced back and forth, voicing her own opinion with an occasional "*R-r-r-ruff.*"

"This time it's more than a mere fuss, believe me." Kim slowly twirled the glass between her fingers. "If the association vote swings in favor of banning animals, a lot of residents will sell out and move, including me. The majority of pet owners have been here since this complex was built. We're more than just friendly neighbors; we've become as close as family and I don't want my family to split up. Some of our elderly residents depend upon their neighbors for help so they can continue to live independently. Who would they turn to if we left?"

Rock frowned as he filled his glass. "With all those units for sale at the same time, the value of everyone's property is bound to decrease."

"Including yours." Kim sipped her champagne and waited for that little tidbit to sink in.

Rock looked her straight in the eye. "Perhaps there's a way we can accommodate each other."

She froze, suspending the flute midway to her lips as her suspicion grew. It always came down to sex, didn't it? Men didn't have anything else on their minds. "If you're suggesting that I sleep with you as a tradeoff—"

"No, no." He waved away the notion. "Just live with me for about a week. I need your help."

What did he have in mind—a live-in maid with a little hanky-panky on the side? Did he really think she'd fall for that lie? Her disgust boiled over.

"Get out of my house, Rock Henderson!" She scooped up Sasha and jumped to her feet. The dog wriggled from her grasp and landed on the loveseat cushion, barking as it dived to the floor and raced out of sight. "This conversation is over."

She tossed the last swallow of champagne into his face and stormed out of the room.

*   *   *

Rock snatched the silk handkerchief from his front pocket and mopped his chin before the sticky liquid dripped onto his jacket.

Huh...that went well.

A moment later, Kim's bedroom door slammed, reminding him that he needed her in his bedroom. Tonight.

"Ah, c'mon, Kim," he coaxed gently as he crossed the room and rapped his knuckle on the door. "I didn't mean it the way it sounded. I'm sorry if I made you upset."

"Apology accepted," she said, sounding tired, but deliberate. "Now, go home."

"I'm not leaving until you come out and give me a chance to explain." He tried the knob and found it locked. "Besides, there's at least two more glasses of champagne left and I hate drinking alone."

The tree lights suddenly flickered and went dark. He glanced over his shoulder just in time to catch that mutt with the cord between its teeth, pulling the plug out of the wall.

"Hey, you, stop that!" He walked over to the tree and knelt to rescue the dog, but snatched his hand back before the ungrateful little critter could sink a mouthful of pointy teeth into his thumb. "You keep chewing on that cord, Half-Pint, and I guarantee you're going to turn into a grilled sausage, fully charred."

Behind him, the bedroom door flew open and Kim rushed to his side, gasping in horror. "Let go of the cord, baby!" She pried the apparatus from Sasha's mouth and snatched the dog into her arms. Without a word, she turned to head back into her boudoir, but Rock stepped in her path, nearly causing her to collide with his chest. The top of her head barely reached his chin and she couldn't have weighed more than one hundred ten pounds soaking wet. Wrapped in all that pink fluff, she looked more like a ball of cotton candy than a tough-as-nails nurse practitioner.

She looked up, her gaze boring into his. "You're blocking my way."

"Just a minute." He gripped his hands on his hips, unwilling to let her pass until he'd made his point. "I just saved your pooch from getting barbecued and that's all you have to say?"

"You're right," she answered with a begrudging smile. "Thank you." As she attempted to skirt around him, he cupped her elbow, steering her toward the living room.

"You're welcome. Now, can we please start over?" Rock lowered his voice to a gentler tone. "You said you needed my help." He gestured toward the twin loveseats. "Let's sit down. I have a proposal to make and I promise I won't bite, though I can't say the same for your mutt...er, baby."

As if it understood, the mangy little cur rolled back its top lip, silently showing him a set of sharp fangs.

Rock cleared his throat and shoved his hands into his pockets. After the day he'd endured, he could use a nice, stiff shot about now, but preferably not tetanus.

He nodded toward the living room. "Shall we?"

Kim hesitated, as if weighing her options. "All right," she replied with a sigh, "but don't try coming on to me again or I'll sic my dog on you."

He agreed and followed her back to the loveseats, taking his previous spot.

"Now," he continued in a business tone, "I want you to listen with an open mind until I'm finished." He took a deep breath and braced himself. Might as well cut to the chase and get it out there. "I really do need you to move in with me for about a week...and pretend to be my wife."

Her jaw dropped. "Excuse me?"

The sudden chill in the air almost made him shudder as she sat up straight, mirroring the image of an ice sculpture he'd once viewed at the St. Paul Winter Carnival. Her wide blue eyes regarded him with skepticism and distrust. He studied her for a moment, wondering what to say next. Her blonde pixie cut, upturned nose and smattering of freckles fit the image of the proverbial girl next door. She'd probably make a great wife for the right guy one of these days. However, did she possess the skill to convince Zelda that she would be the perfect wife for him?

"Let's have another drink." Rock grabbed the bottle and began to pour, filling her flute. "I'll start from the beginning."

"Please do." Her lips barely moved, the words slipping out in monosyllables.

"A couple months ago I became engaged. That was my first mistake." He set the bottle down and clasped his hands together. "Then I told my mother."

"What's wrong with telling your mom? That's usually the first person you call to announce good news." Kim picked up her bubbling flute. "I gather you're not engaged any longer."

"No." He rubbed his palm over his emerging five-o-clock shadow. "She didn't work out."

Kim didn't comment, but her raised eyebrows suggested she didn't empathize with someone who talked about breaking up with his future wife like a business deal gone bad.

"Okay, there's more to it than *that*. She double-crossed me."

"She cheated on you?"

"It's on par with infidelity as far as I'm concerned." His shook his head, still angry about it. "She obtained confidential information through intimate conversations with me and turned it over to my competitor. Of course, when I discovered the leak and confronted her, she professed extreme remorse. According to her," he paused, replaying the scene in his mind, "by that time, she had allegedly realized she'd fallen in love with me."

"What does all this have to do with me getting your vote?"

"I didn't tell my family what happened once the engagement ended." He gave a cynical laugh. "My mother would've been so disappointed she would have never let me hear the end of it." Squaring his shoulders, he downed his drink in three gulps and set the flute on the table. "Now that the wedding date has passed and no one received an invitation, everyone thinks I eloped."

Kim burst into incredulous laughter. "Why don't you just tell them the truth, Mr. Chief Executive Hypocrite? You didn't like being deceived, so why are you deceiving them?"

Because you don't disappoint Zelda, he thought glumly. Especially the way things stood now.

"My mother's heart is in bad shape. I'm afraid of what it would do

9

to her if I told her what really happened. She's so happy now that she thinks I'm married."

"How is putting on a charade going to keep her happy? She'll find out eventually and then you'll have to account for lying to her, too."

"She's not going to last much longer, so I don't see the point in causing her any more pain than she's already bearing." Rock grabbed Kim's glass and consumed her champagne, wishing he could just tell his mother the truth. Unfortunately, life didn't work that way. "If she's going to die soon then all I want is for her to go happy."

"You don't actually believe you're going to pull this off, do you? I mean, I'm not the vain, self-centered type that you date. I don't know how to act haughty and spoiled. She's going to see right through me." Kim set her dog aside and stood up. "Forget it."

Desperation fueled his frustration. Rock stood to his full height, towering over her. "Look, you don't have to be my type; you just have to be by my side for a week. I've got everything covered."

"*If* I agree to it, I'm not moving in with you."

Heat began to build under his collar. "Oh, yes, you are, *darlin'*. The last time I checked, that's the way married couples operated."

"But we're not married. We're not even working out at the gym together." She rose up on her tiptoes and poked him in the chest with her index finger. "So if you think I'm going to sleep in the same bed with you—"

He leaned forward and grabbed her hand. A surge of attraction coursed through him as he covered her petite fingers with his broad palm. It threw him off guard for a moment, but the prospect of spending the night with her suddenly intrigued him. "What's the matter, darlin', are you afraid you might like sleeping with me?"

Her eyes narrowed as she jerked her hand away. "Get over yourself, Rock Henderson. What I'm afraid of is that you wouldn't be able to control your ego long enough to last an entire evening without sex."

"Don't worry about that. You're not my type—remember? I'll be a perfect gentleman. Besides, before you know it, the week will be over. Look, I can't disappoint my mother. If you want my vote, those are my terms. No *wifey*," he pointed at her mutt, "no doggie."

She clamped her jaw shut. After a few tense moments of staring him down, she said through clenched teeth, "When is *Mother* scheduled to arrive?"

His stomach churned. "She showed up this afternoon with her nurse." He grabbed the champagne bottle by the neck, brought it to his lips and drained the last few drops. The champagne went down like water, but it did little to relieve his apprehension.

"I had no idea that she'd planned this visit. She decided to surprise me and lay over a few days in Minneapolis before flying to Vail to spend Christmas with my brother, Patrick. She wanted to meet my wife! I didn't know what to do until I remembered my assistant telling me you had left messages with her saying that you desperately needed *my* help. So I decided to pay you a visit and see if we could strike a deal. I couldn't get away earlier to talk to you about it because I had to take Mother out to dinner. I told her you couldn't make it because you were out for the day shopping with your girlfriends."

His BlackBerry suddenly buzzed. He glanced at the screen and turned it off. "It's her. I'd better go. She's probably wondering why it's taking so long to get a newspaper. How soon can you change and come upstairs?"

She gave him a stubborn look. "I didn't say I'd do it, yet. I've been looking forward to taking a vacation at Christmastime for years. Do you have any idea how long it took me to gain enough seniority at the hospital to get this week off? I have gifts to buy, parties to attend and lunch dates with friends. Playing house with you isn't my idea of a vacation!"

11

"Yeah, but you did say that the fate of your residency here and all your long-time neighbors is hanging on my vote. You hold all the cards…"

"But, Rock, I don't have the expensive designer clothes that your fiancé would wear. I live in scrubs and a lab coat. You know that."

He shrugged. "The day I showed my fiancé the door, she departed in such a rage that she left some clothes in my closet—mostly things I bought." He looked her over. "She's taller, but you're about her size. Just wear hers. They'll look better on you than they did on her, anyway."

He set the empty bottle back on the coffee table and headed for the door. Pausing with his hand on the doorknob, he turned back. "I'll tell Mother you're on your way home and due to arrive any minute. Oh, and by the way, your name is Diona Daye. Got that?"

"What?" She stomped across the room. "You mean I have to change my name, too? What are we going to do when someone sees me in the lobby and calls me Kim?"

"I don't know. We'll just make sure no one sees us together. At any rate, let's concentrate on one issue at a time, like getting through the next hour or two." He reached into his trouser pocket. "Here's your security card for the elevator. It's also my private entrance into the garage. You can move your car tomorrow."

Something caught his eye. He glanced down as she slowly took the card. "Hey," he remarked with a wide grin, "are those bunny slippers on your feet? I haven't seen anyone wearing those since I was about ten years old."

"Yeah." She stuck out her chin. "Gee, is that a tux you're wearing? I haven't seen anyone show up for a meeting with me in one of those *ever*."

She sure was cute, but he knew better than to verbalize it.

He opened the door a crack and peered out at the empty hallway before looking back at her. "My company Christmas bash is going on tonight at the Hilton. It's too bad I had to miss my own party, but Mother didn't feel up to going. It cost a small fortune." He gave her a wink, determined to let it go and concentrate on the issue at hand. "See you in a few minutes, *Diona*."

The throw pillow intended for his head hit the backside of the door as he slipped out and hustled toward the stairwell. Kim's spunky temper felt like a refreshing breeze compared to Diona's constant pouting. He exhaled absently; relieved that he'd caught on to Diona's traitorous scheme before she'd caused too much damage to his company. Even so, she'd still managed to ruin his belief in marriage and proved beyond a doubt that he couldn't trust anyone with either his deepest secrets or with his heart. He had no idea if he'd ever meet someone who would change his mind, but for now, he planned to live his life one day at a time, leaving the past behind.

He slipped into the stairwell and bounded down the stairs to make it to the lobby and get on his own elevator, all the while wondering if Kim would hit it off with Zelda or if his mother would see right through her pretense. Time would tell, but one thing seemed certain. No matter how well Kim played her part, it would take a miracle to get through this week—with both women.

Chapter 2

Later that evening...

Classical music and soft lighting enveloped Kim as she stepped out of Rock's private elevator and stared in amazement at the palatial opulence of her temporary home. Pivoting slowly, she took in the oyster white walls and black marble flooring of the circular foyer. A large drum table set with a vase of fresh flowers stood majestically upon an ice blue silk rug in the center of the room. Overhead, a chandelier of hand-blown glass held six shimmering candelabras between alternating scrolls of delicate rose-colored flowers and leaves.

She stared wistfully, taking in every detail of a privileged lifestyle she'd never before experienced and, after this week, wouldn't likely enjoy again. From what she already knew of Rock Henderson, he spent his professional life in boardrooms and country clubs, making decisions that affected his company's bottom line. Gossip around the building described his personal life as rivaling that of a movie star, with staff to attend to his every whim. His women were high society, educated at the best colleges and snooty to boot. He had nothing in common with a middle-class nurse practitioner who lived in scrubs and a lab coat and often dined on hospital cafeteria food. He must have been completely out of options to pick such an unlikely person to be his wife!

For the umpteenth time in the last half hour, she wondered if she'd jumped in over her head. Would this be an interesting way to spend her vacation days or a stupid, impulsive mistake that resulted in the week from hell?

Voices echoing from a distant room jerked her thoughts back to reality. She recognized Rock's deep timbre, but not the woman's voice and assumed it must be his mother. Though she couldn't make out their conversation over the music, both had a strong, commanding presence. In other words, both were accustomed to running the show, and from the tone of their voices, they were embroiled in a serious discussion.

She crossed the foyer and ventured down a white hallway, passing several closed doors sandwiched between custom white cabinetry along the walls. Her boots clicked on the stone tile, making her self-conscious of announcing her own arrival. Halfway down the hallway she stopped at an alcove furnished with a black leather bench on one side, a marble-topped table and mirror on the other. She paused to check her outfit. She'd dressed with care, selecting her best pair of designer jeans. The cashmere turtleneck sweater and matching Jimmy Choo dress boots belonged to Candy Kirchoff in unit 303E, borrowed at the last minute. To make it look as though she'd been shopping, Kim wore a white mink jacket and carried a large Saks Fifth Avenue bag. The short, baseball-style fur had been Veronica's favorite gift from one of her past loves. Hopefully, no one would notice the slight wear on the silk and wool blend cuffs. The shopping bag contained pajamas, toiletries, a small plastic bag of dog food and of course, the bunny slippers.

Flushed spots stained her cheeks, betraying her nervousness. Her stomach fluttered like crazy.

Do I look the part? Can I pull this off?

She looked down at her companion peeking through the top of a pink tote. "Well, Sasha, I must be crazy to have agreed to this ridiculous charade, but here we go..."

Squaring her shoulders, she walked toward a large open doorway, her high-heeled boots clicking a loud staccato beat to give Rock plenty of advance notice just in case they were arguing...er, discussing her.

Rock stood with his back to a magnificent wall of windows, ignoring the dramatic nighttime view of the lights along the Mississippi riverfront and the Minneapolis skyline. To his right, a robust fire burned in the hearth. Oak bookcases and white Italian leather furniture lined the wall opposite the windows.

An elderly woman sat in her wheelchair next to the sofa with a glass of sparkling water in her hand, wearing a red wool suit and enough bling to start her own jewelry store. Her nurse, outfitted in a starched white dress, stockings and shoes, stood stoically behind her, gripping the handles of the chair. Most of the woman's pale face, devoid of makeup, hid behind large tortoiseshell glasses. She wore her nut-brown hair parted on the side and twisted into a chignon at her nape. Kim wondered where she came from. No one in the medical profession dressed like that in these parts.

The conversation abruptly ceased when Kim entered the room and all three occupants focused upon her. Her gaze met Rock's stunned silence as he took in her appearance, one curve at a time. Her breath refused to leave her lungs, but she couldn't tell what made her more nervous, the situation with his mother or his shock at seeing her in sexy clothes.

It was show and tell time...

She cleared her throat. "Rock, I—"

"Oh, there you are, darlin'," Rock responded quickly, cutting her off. "We've been waiting for you." He met her in the center of the room and kissed her tenderly on the forehead. His arm encircled her waist, pulling her close as he gazed down at her with adoration. Tremors shot up her spine as his hand caressed her lower back. "Did you have a good time shopping?"

Sasha let out a snort and disappeared inside the carrier.

"Y-yes, I did." His strong grip held her with surprising gentleness. She gazed into his deep brown eyes and swallowed hard. Boy, he sure took this *wifey* thing seriously. "Sorry I'm late," she managed to say, but the words came out in a breathy-sounding squeak. "Ginny and Sarah insisted on having dinner at Roberto's and you know how slow their service can be."

He laughed, making it seem as though Ginny and Sarah were close friends.

"Mother," he said, turning toward the regal woman in the wheelchair, "allow me to introduce my lovely wife, Diona Daye-Henderson." Then to Kim he said, "Diona, meet my mother, Zelda, and her nurse, Marie."

At the announcement of her name, Marie went as rigid as a post. Instead of extending her palm to shake, she simply stood with white-knuckled hands gripping the chair and stared at Kim.

"Marie doesn't speak English," Zelda stated with a dismissive wave of her hand.

Kim set her bags on the floor and extended her hand, forcing herself to hold it steady. "It's a pleasure to meet you, Zelda. Rock has told me so much about you." *As much as he could divulge in five minutes, anyway.*

"The pleasure is mine," Zelda replied with a slight British accent. Her throaty voice, though authoritative, sounded slightly raspy. Her thick white hair, styled short in a razor cut, gave her rectangular face a distinguished look. Her full red lips pursed together as her sharp-eyed gaze examined every inch of the new Mrs. Henderson. She took Kim's hand and gripped it firmly. "My goodness," she exclaimed as she examined Kim's naked fingers, "where's your wedding ring?"

Rock's face drained whiter than the starched collar of his shirt. "Ah…" he said and looked down at Kim, obviously stalling until he came up with a plausible excuse. "It's…ah…it's at the jewelers. The bands didn't fit right so we needed to have them re-sized. We wouldn't want her to lose it swimming in the ocean on our next romantic getaway, now would we?"

Zelda gave him a mother's stare, silently communicating that she had a good mind to smack him across the back of the head for smarting off. After a tense moment, however, she let it go and turned back to Kim. "In any case, I'm delighted to finally meet you, Diona." She launched another disapproving glance at Rock. "My son has been keeping you a secret and I don't understand why."

Rock's arm tightened around Kim's waist. "Mother, I've already explained this to you. We went to Vegas for the weekend and on the spur of the moment, tied the knot. That's all. There is no sinister plot to keep our marriage from you."

"Las Vegas, of all places!" Zelda's steel blue eyes flashed brighter than her dazzling diamond studs and she leaned her stout frame forward in her chair, as though she might jump out of it at any moment. "What a disgrace to the institution of marriage! I supposed you went to one of those cheesy little chapels where they play canned music and pin a two-dollar corsage on the bride. Did Elvis perform the ceremony, too?"

"We don't need a big, fancy wedding to have a good life together," Rock implored and gazed down at Kim. "Do we, darlin'?"

The tone of his last sentence plainly indicated he wanted her agreement *now*. Rock had her by the waist, Zelda had her by the hand—a Henderson family 'how-do-you-do' tug-of-war. This did not bode well for a fun-filled week. Kim drew in a deep breath to speak, but Zelda beat her to it.

"Rubbish," Zelda snapped. "You will have a proper wedding in the church. I'll speak to our clergy about it right away. After all," she clutched the almond-sized diamond pendant hovering over her heart, "I'm not going to be around much longer. I want to leave this life knowing that at least one of my sons is happily situated. That's my dying wish." Zelda lifted her chin and stared pointedly at her son. "Well, that and a few grandchildren."

She wants a few grandchildren? Kim blinked in horror. Rock hadn't mentioned anything about that. Just how long did she plan to hang on, anyway?

Rock's muscles tensed as though Zelda's announcement had taken him by surprise, too. A large vein on his neck began pulsing erratically. Kim tugged her hand from Zelda's grasp and placed it on his chest. "A church wedding would be wonderful," she said to Rock in a sugary sweet voice, though his mother was the intended target. "But there's no hurry since we're already married. Let's just enjoy Christmas as a family and wait until after the holidays to talk about future plans."

Rock glared at her, the sizzle in his gaze conveying the message, "*What do you think you're doing?*"

She ignored him and turned to Zelda. "A fabulous wedding, if done properly, takes at least a year to plan. Don't you agree?"

Zelda looked flustered, as though she had not expected Diona to receive her demands with so much enthusiasm. "I—of course. If you want everything to be perfect, I suppose you'd need that much time. The farther out you place the date, the more likely your wedding planner will be able to retain the reception hall of your choosing and the best service providers."

Kim nodded, knowing she had given the old lady exactly what she wanted. "Then let's wait until after the holidays when we can give it our full attention and decide on a date that satisfies everyone."

Rock nuzzled his lips into her hair. "You'd better have a good explanation for this..."

Kim smiled innocently. Why should she care? He was the one who'd created this mess. She wasn't going to be here long, anyway. After she got his vote, the wedding plans were his problem.

"Well..." Zelda said and stared at her son again. "I don't know if I can hang on that long. We'll talk about it again before I leave. We don't have to decide tonight." She waved a bejeweled hand toward the sofa and motioned Kim to take a seat. "Come here and sit down so we can chat. I'd like to get to know you better." She pointed at her son. "Rock, be a gentleman and take her coat. Where are your manners?"

Kim unzipped her jacket and allowed Rock to remove it, his long, deft fingers sliding across the fine fabric of her sweater, caressing her arms as he slid the fur off her shoulders. Never mind, she told herself and dismissed the giddiness in her stomach. He could put on the devoted husband act to impress his mother, but if he intended to turn his attentiveness into seduction once they were alone, he was in for a surprise.

Zelda shoved an empty stemmed glass at the nurse and spoke curtly to her in French. The tall, willowy woman didn't argue, but the way she pursed her lips and stomped toward the kitchen spoke volumes about her attitude of taking orders like household help.

Zelda turned to Kim. "She's fetching me a fresh glass of Perrier. I told her to refresh the wine as well. Would you like a glass?"

Kim nodded and handed Rock her shopping bag then gingerly took a seat on the sofa, feeling like a bug under a microscope. She set Sasha's carrier on the floor next to her. As soon as it landed on the plush carpet, Sasha began to yip through the mesh window.

Zelda raised her brows and looked warily at the floor. "Is that a dog in your bag?"

"Yes, it's my Chihuahua. I apologize for the racket she's making. She's just excited to have company." Kim leaned forward and reached into the bag, stroking the dog's sleek coat. "Hush, Sasha!"

"My word, but she's a tiny thing," Zelda remarked and peered at the wet, button-like nose peeking through the opening, sniffing the air. She extended her hand to pet the dog, but snatched it back when Sasha responded with a low, frightened growl. "Oh! She snapped at me!"

Mortified, Kim placed her hand into the bag again to calm the dog. Of all the things to go wrong, this should not have topped the list!

"I'm sorry, Zelda," she said in a rush, even though Sasha had not actually attempted to bite, but instead had shrunk back at the intrusion of a strange hand in her portable bed. "I don't know what's come over her. She never reacts to women that way."

The nurse returned with a tray containing two wine glasses and Zelda's water. Kim reached for a glass, but her fingers barely wrapped around the stem when the tray moved and the wine sloshed, spilling over on her hand. She could have sworn the nurse did that on purpose, but let it go and smiled sweetly. "Thank you, Marie."

The nurse ignored her. Instead, Marie fixed her gaze on the hallway where Rock had disappeared to hang Kim's coat in the foyer closet.

"This is wonderful Riesling," Kim said after downing an unladylike gulp, desperate to calm her frayed nerves.

Zelda gave her a puzzled look. "It's not Riesling; that's Chardonnay."

Oops. Kim stared at her glass, too embarrassed to look up. "You're right. I don't drink much white wine, except the sparkling kind. Mostly, I prefer red."

"That's odd," Zelda remarked in a questioning tone. "My son prefers white, like I do. Rather, like I used to. I find it interesting that you and he have opposite tastes."

"Well, you know what they say," Kim countered with a sheepish giggle. "Opposites attract." Her answer sounded as inadequate as she felt, but she couldn't take it back now.

The nurse leaned over and whispered something in Zelda's ear. Rock's mother whispered something back, nodded to her and then turned to Kim as Marie watched the doorway, presumably waiting for Rock to come back. "So, my dear, I understand you're related to the Daye family of Martha's Vineyard. What is your relationship to Arnie and Barb?"

Who?

Kim panicked, wondering how much Zelda knew about the real Diona Daye, but without Rock around to add his two cents, she had to punt this time. "Um...they're my aunt and uncle."

"Really?" Zelda's steel gray eyes became beacons. "They used to be neighbors of mine before my late husband passed away. Strange, but I don't recall ever hearing them speak of your mother. Her name is...?"

"Veronica," Kim blurted without thinking, "but you probably have never heard of us because we only saw them once a year at a family picnic, er, reunion."

That much rang true. Veronica had family in Martha's Vineyard, but she'd become estranged from her parents before Kim's birth and only came back to visit a friend and one cousin once a year.

"I see." Zelda sipped her water, her mouth prim. "Well, next time you see Arnie, tell that dear old chap to ring me up. I'd love to hear from him."

"I will," Kim replied and suddenly focused all her attention on sipping her wine.

"I'm curious," Zelda continued. "If your family is from New England, how did you end up in Minnesota?"

"I went to the University."

Zelda leaned forward. "Why did you pick this one? Why not Radisson or Smith? Certainly you could have attended a higher caliber school than what Minnesota has to offer."

That remark stung, but Kim resisted the urge to get upset. "My best friend and I came here together. She had an athletic scholarship and I just wanted to go somewhere new. At the time, it seemed like the right thing to do and I've never looked back. After all, if I would have gone to a private college out east, I'd have never met Rock."

Zelda pursed her lips, clearly showing her difference of opinion.

"What sorority did you belong to?"

Kim's smile froze. Sorority? "Um..." she faltered, thinking furiously. "Delta Nu?" Her voice wavered, sounding shrill.

Marie coughed and turned away. Did she just roll her eyes? Things were going downhill fast if even the nurse could sense her panic.

"And what is your degree?"

"I have an MFA, majoring in art history." Not really, but it sounded glamorous, like something the real Diona Daye might choose.

"Where does one work after receiving such a degree?"

"She doesn't need to work outside our home," Rock broke in as he re-entered the living room. "She has plenty to do here, taking care of me and handling the entertaining of my clients."

With anyone else, Kim would have bristled at such a sexist comment, but given the situation, she breathed a silent sigh of relief and welcomed his matter-of-fact tone, making it plain she didn't need to answer the question.

Zelda scrutinized the two of them, as though she enjoyed interrogating them. "But, how did you meet?"

"Through a friend," Rock replied.

"At an association meeting about a year ago," Kim said at the same time. Everyone stared at her. "I live—I mean I *used* to own a condo on the sixth floor. Rock was dating a mutual friend who also lives in the building and she introduced us."

In truth, Shelly Gartner didn't count as a genuine friend and her only motivation for introducing Rock to Kim that day centered exclusively on showing off her golden catch to every woman at the meeting, but neither Rock nor Zelda needed to know that now. Rock had quickly tired of Shelly, anyway, leaving the vain witch to swallow her pride and cry in the fancy eighteen-dollar Cosmopolitans she regularly consumed.

Sasha's steady growling became impossible to ignore. Kim tried to quiet the dog by gently stroking her back, but Sasha wouldn't settle down.

Zelda looked around the apartment and grunted with distaste. "Well, I suggest you sell this expensive attic and buy something more sensible. My son needs a home with a beautiful garden and room for children to play. I know just the property in St. Petersburg and I'll set up an appointment with my agent for you to view it when you come to visit me in February on my birthday."

Rock seized the last glass of wine from the nurse's tray and turned to Zelda. "Now, Mother, there's nothing wrong with this penthouse. It's an investment. It cost me a cool million and I'm—we're quite happy here." Sasha's yipping nearly drowned out his voice. He looked at Kim and shouted, "Aren't we, darlin'?"

Suddenly a large orange and gold tabby strutted out from behind Zelda's wheelchair. He stopped in the center of the group and looked around as though surveying his new territory.

Sasha's barking escalated into uncontrollable shrieking. The tabby sauntered over to the bag and peered through the mesh window. With an angry hiss, he slashed his paw at the mesh, slicing through the fabric. Sasha jumped out of the bag, howling like a demon and took off running. The tabby shot after her, charging right between the nurse's legs.

Marie screamed and dropped the tray. It sailed to the floor like a Frisbee, bouncing around on Rock's sky blue carpeting.

"Roscoe, come back here!" Zelda shouted. Then she turned and barked at her nurse, "Fetch him!" She repeated the order in French, but the nurse merely pursed her lips and backed away.

Turning to her son, Zelda said, "Rock, my poor pussy cat has been upset by that nasty little dog! Go rescue him!"

Something crashed in the other room—something apparently glass and delicate, by the splintering sound piercing the air. Rock and Kim rushed toward the dining area and found Roscoe perched atop the table next to a shattered crystal bud vase and a pool of water dripping onto the hardwood floor, his tail twitching with evil delight.

Kim made sure they were out of earshot before grabbing Rock by the arm. "Why didn't you tell me your mother brought her cat?" she whispered.

He stared at the snarling feline with a baffled expression. "I didn't know she had one."

Kim took stock of the situation and shook her head. First, Mommy Dearest had subjected her to the third degree and now that monster cat was trying to slice and dice her baby. Welcome to the family...

*   *   *

Rock tossed back the rest of his wine and discarded the empty glass on the only dry spot on his dining room table. He'd had enough disasters for one day. That screeching little mongrel cowering in the corner turned what could have been a pleasant evening into three-ring circus. As for that flea-bitten, germ-bag of a cat...

"Get off my table, fur ball," he said and tried to nudge Roscoe with his knuckle. Angered by the intrusion, the huge tabby yowled and bit down hard on the crook of his finger.

"O-w-w-w-w-w!"

Roscoe dived off the table, landing on the floor with a heavy thud then made a beeline for Sa...Sa... Rock couldn't remember the ankle biter's name, but it sounded a lot like...sausage. He chased the cat into the kitchen and almost lost his balance when he tried to hop over a pile of fresh Tootsie Rolls, Chihuahua style. Murmuring a few choice expletives, he looked around for the dog and found her cowering in the corner, trembling in fear as the tabby advanced, baring his teeth. Rock swooped down and scooped up Kim's pooch before The Striped

Terminator could turn it into a taco dinner. The dog's soft belly fit in the palm of his hand like a water-filled balloon, but when he lifted it off the floor, it suddenly sprang a leak. A stream of liquid cascaded to his shoe and spattered all over the stone tile.

"It's not her fault," Kim snapped as she snatched the dog from him. "How would you feel if you were being ambushed by a tomcat so mean he made Stephen King movies look like cartoons?" She glanced at the dog's double accident. "Tell me where the cleaning supplies are and I'll take care of the mess right away."

Hmmm, where were the cleaning supplies? He glanced around the kitchen, scanning the natural oak cabinetry, stainless steel appliances and black marble countertops. "I don't know. They must be here somewhere. My housekeeper uses them every day."

He stomped his foot. "Scat, Roscoe. Go back to the living room and hide under the couch. Act totally useless, like a normal tomcat." The tabby tore out of the kitchen meowing in protest, his large stomach lurching from side to side.

Kim placed The Sausage on a bar stool and moved briskly about the kitchen, opening doors to find the cleaning supplies.

Rock glanced over his shoulder to make sure he wouldn't be overheard. "Don't take this personally," he offered gently, "but have patience with Zelda. I know she's a little abrupt. That's just her way."

"She's a *little* abrupt?" Kim opened a narrow closet door and stopped. "Rock, I don't mean to be critical of your mother, but she's about as tactful as a cop maintaining crowd control." She pulled out a mop and bucket. "She wants grandchildren. Like, yesterday!"

"Can you blame her? She's dying." Rock stood behind her, placing his hands on her arms. "Just humor her, okay? It's only for a few days." Her shoulder blades fit comfortably under the span of his hands. He squeezed gently. She stopped and turned her head, her wide blue eyes gazing up at him. Her full lips sparkled with cherry-scented gloss. He bent closer, contemplating breaking their agreement as a simple thought grew into an impulsive urge to kiss her.

His BlackBerry buzzed in the pocket of his jacket. He pulled it out.

"This is Rock," he said gruffly, expecting the caller to be one of his managers wondering why he'd ditched his own Christmas party. Only a few people knew this number so it surprised him when he heard the security guard's gravelly voice.

"Ever'thing okay up there, Mr. Henderson?"

"Sure, Al," Rock said as Kim broke away.

"Is that Al Grabowski?" At Rock's affirmative nod she added, "Does he need his blood pressure checked? I monitor it for him once a week."

When Rock shook his head, she turned away and began filling the bucket in the sink. He pulled off his wet shoe and set it on the lid of a chrome trashcan. "Everything is just ho-ho-ho. Why do you want to know?"

"Sorry to bother you so late in the evenin'," Al said. "I got a call from the Robertsons in the unit below yours. They said they were out on their balcony havin' a smoke and thought they heard a scream comin' from your place."

Rock leaned against the counter and toed off his other patent leather shoe. He always kept his patio doors cracked an inch or so for fresh air whenever he had the fireplace going. "It's nothing to worry about, just a little turf war between the dog and the cat."

"When did you get a dog and a cat?" Al's voice echoed loudly with concern. "Don't you know there's a moratorium until the January meetin' on bringin' in any new animals? Did you check with the association first?"

"Don't worry, Al, neither one of them are mine," Rock replied with a wry laugh. Not in a million years... "I have guests for the holidays. My mother and her nurse are staying with me for a few days and I found out the hard way that she brought her cat along for a visit, too. It didn't sit well with my other guest's dog."

"Oh, you mean Miss Kim?"

Rock started with surprise, nearly dropping the phone. He lowered his voice. "How did you know she brought her dog up to my place?"

Kim leaned against the mop, listening.

"I know ever'thing that goes on around here, Mr. Henderson. That's my job."

There were security cameras on every floor. Over time, Al Grabowski, the senior security manager, must have collected enough dirt on the residents of this building to start his own reality show.

"I'll call the Robertsons, Al, and assure them everything is fine."

"That won't be necessary, Mr. Henderson. I'll take care of that. Y'all have a nice evenin'."

Rock hung up at the same time Zelda bellowed his name. He shoved the BlackBerry into his pocket as he hurried into the living room. "Mother, are you all right?"

"As good as I can be, given the circumstances." She shifted uncomfortably in her chair then motioned for Marie to take her to her bedroom. "I'm going to bed. I've an important errand to run tomorrow." She shook her finger at him. "You're taking me shopping to buy a wedding present for your bride."

"You don't need to go to all that trouble, Mother." The words came blundering out before he could stop himself. "I mean, you've just arrived. There's no hurry."

"Why not?" She sent him a hard, piercing look. "Is there some reason why I shouldn't buy your wife a gift?"

Her question, leveled like a rap on the knuckles, stopped him in his tracks. "We're expecting snow tomorrow. It's going to be cold and slippery. You should stay inside where it's warm and get some rest. We'll have plenty of time for shopping once the storm passes."

"I may be in a wheelchair, but I'm not senile!" She shook her fist as the nurse sped her away. "I can bloody well make my own decisions! Get some *sleep* and be ready to go first thing in the morning. I want coffee at seven o'clock sharp."

Rock watched his white-haired mother disappear down the hallway. Sleep? With any luck, he wouldn't get a wink. But first, he had to find out if Kim intended to keep him at an arm's length or if she was simply bluffing about sharing his bed like a good little make-believe wife. He smiled, wondering what it would be like to cuddle her soft, curvy body in his arms.

Let the chase begin...

Chapter 3

Nighty night...

With Sasha nestled in the crook of her arm, Kim entered the living room to face Zelda again. Instead, she found Rock leaning on one hand against the fireplace mantle, staring at the flames with a silly grin. What could possibly have caused him to be so amused? So far, this evening had proved to be anything but funny.

"Where's your mother? I thought she wanted to interrogate me some more."

He grabbed the remote and extinguished the fire. "She went to bed, but I've been given strict orders to have her coffee ready first thing in the morning. We'll have to go out for breakfast. Dora, my housekeeper and cook, has the week off." He set the remote back on the coffee table and turned to her, all serious now. "You look unhappy. Is something wrong?"

Kim took a deep breath. "Yes, there's a lot wrong," she whispered. "We have a dog and cat that don't get along, we have a nurse who doesn't understand English, we have a sham of a marriage that's based on nothing but a bunch of lies, and those lies, Rock, are going to multiply each day until we can't keep our story straight any more. Now that I've met your mother, I just don't know if this is best for her. She's making an awful lot of plans centered on two people who don't intend to see them through. It's not right to deceive her. I don't feel good about it."

He gripped her by the shoulders. "What's so wrong about giving her the thing she wants the most? If she dies a happy woman believing I have a solid marriage then it will all be worth it."

"But what if she doesn't die? What if—God willing—she survives another five years?"

"Then I'll have to tell her the truth. After all, there won't be any reason to grant her last wish, will there? It's getting late. We should probably turn in." He placed his hand firmly on her elbow. "Shall we?"

They reached the doorway of his bedroom at the end of the hallway and Sasha began wriggling, impatient to get back on solid ground. Kim set the dog on the floor, scooting her through the entrance to get her inside before Zelda's cat appeared out of nowhere again and caused another ruckus.

"I'll open a fresh bottle of wine," Rock said, activating the lamps on the twin nightstands flanking his king-sized bed. "Would you like a glass?"

"No, thank you." She waved her hand, distracted as she watched Sasha trot around the room, sniffing the carpet then disappear under the bed. "I'd rather have a Perrier."

Concern over the possibility of Sasha nervously soiling the velvety beige carpeting with doggie-do kept her so preoccupied she didn't object when Rock shut the door and flipped a wall switch, filling the room with soft music. Before she could get her thoughts in order, he spun her around and drew her into his arms, engulfing her with a deep kiss.

Stunned at first, she stood frozen to the spot, her mind jumbling as the heat of his mouth melted into hers. Musk and sandalwood aromas of his cologne filled her head, clouding her thoughts. For a moment, she forgot to breathe. Then she drew in a sharp breath, inhaling his manly scent. Deft fingers ignited a trail of fireworks as his hand slid down her spine and rested on the small of her back, pressing her close to him.

Wow...

Instinctively, she slid her arms around his neck and leaned into the kiss, savoring the apple and vanilla flavors of Chardonnay reserve on his lips. She heard a sigh escape her throat as his strong arms surrounded her, pulling her closer to his chest. Something in the way he held her—so confident, yet so tender—pierced her heart and in that moment, she knew that to possess the devotion of a man so loving would be all that a woman like her would ever need.

Double wow...

Suddenly, an old, familiar scene disrupted her thoughts as it flickered through her mind like a snapshot fluttering in the wind. The image of a beautiful woman locked in her lover's embrace lasted only a moment, but it resurrected powerful memories of Kim's childhood and the heartbroken tears of a lonely, forgotten little girl.

I'm acting like a tramp—just like Veronica.

Her eyelids flew open.

Kim gasped and slammed her palms against his chest, pushing herself away. "Just what do you think you're doing?"

Rock went still, his dark eyes filled with confusion, but he quickly recovered and chuckled, placing his hands on her shoulders with a wry grin. "Well, if I have to explain it to you, darlin', I must be doing something wrong."

"Ha-ha, real funny, Casanova." Shoving Veronica's memory to the back of her mind, she backed away from his reach, still shaken from the desire he'd stirred within her. Unlike her mother, she didn't intend to lose control. However, it made her mad to know that he probably just decided to take his chances to see how far he could get. "How dare you take advantage of me like this? We had a deal and if you think I'm going to let one killy sis go to my head—" She folded her arms into a tight bow, embarrassed to have him see her so flustered. "I mean, if you think one *silly kiss* is going to go to my head, you're sadly mistaken!

I agreed to play lovey-dovey in front of your mother, but when we're alone, I'm simply the neighbor in 601E who wants your vote and nothing more. Do you understand?"

"Ah, come on, darlin'," he insisted, as though her words made him feel like a fool. "Don't take it personal. It was just a goodnight kiss."

"Goodnight kiss, my—my foot! You were trying to seduce me!"

"Okay, okay, don't get upset." He raised his palms, signaling a truce. "I thought you'd like it, but if that's not the case, I guarantee it won't happen again. The last thing I want to do is make you unhappy. From now on, I'll be as trustworthy as a Boy Scout."

Kim gave him an arch look. "I can't imagine you in short pants and a neckerchief."

He smiled proudly and held up two fingers, the Boy Scouts of America official salute. "For your information, I made it all the way to Eagle Scout."

His reaction looked so sincere she couldn't resist a wry chuckle. "All right, Rock. In that case, I'll give you one more chance, but don't ever try it again or I'm out of here."

She glanced around his bedroom, an area larger than her living room, furnished with fine Tuscany furniture, ivory walls and beige carpeting. "Now, where am I going to sleep?"

He made a grand sweep of his hand toward the massive four-poster bed covered with a thick brown and blue striped comforter. "Pick your preference, either side. It doesn't matter to me."

She pointed toward the camelback loveseat with four oversized throw pillows covered in the same two-toned print as the comforter. "That should do just fine."

He shrugged. "Well, that thing is all right for sitting on to tie my shoes, but the leather back is cold and though the cushion has fabric on one side, it's hard and too short to be comfortable, even for a pixie like you. You're going to wake up with a sore back from sleeping like a pretzel." When she sighed with disappointment, he put one arm around her shoulder and turned her toward his bed. "I've got the best mattress money can buy. It's like sleeping on a cloud. Go ahead, try it for yourself."

"All right," she said reluctantly, but detoured first to the loveseat, snatching the throw pillows. "I'll take the side nearest the door. You can sleep by the windows." She carried the throw pillows over to the bed, laying them end-to-end down the middle.

"What's that for?" He said as he untied his bowtie and pulled it off.

"I'm setting some boundaries," Kim replied and commenced to plump the pillows.

Sasha began to jump against the side of the bed, trying to scale it.

"You don't have to do that." Rock stuffed his bowtie into his pocket as he collapsed onto the loveseat and began to peel off his socks. "I told you I'd keep to myself from now on."

"Oh, yes, I do." Kim picked up the dog and set her on the bed. "I don't want to be mistaken in the middle of the night for your former girlfriend, especially after you've had a few glasses of wine." Sasha found a comfortable spot on one of the throw pillows and curled up.

Meanwhile, Kim picked up her Saks Fifth Avenue bag and dumped the contents on the bed. She stared at the items strewn about in front of her. "Oh, crap."

Rock arose from the loveseat and came to her side. "What's the matter?"

She made a tsk sound, annoyed with herself. "I forgot Sasha's litter box."

He stared at the assortment of clothes and cosmetics on the bed. "Her...what?"

34

"Sasha is trained to do her business in a plastic box filled with organic material. That way she doesn't have accidents when I'm at work." She sighed and rubbed the back of her neck, beginning to feel the stress of the day. "Well, I'd better run down to my place and get it. She has to go pretty early in the morning."

Rock pulled off his jacket and paused. "Would you mind taking off those noisy boots? Mother might hear you get on the elevator. If she does, she'll be asking a lot of questions tomorrow."

With a nod, Kim sat on the floor and unzipped her leather boots, happy to get those tight things off her feet. No wonder Candy said she could keep them as long as she wanted.

She slipped barefoot out the door and tiptoed down the hallway, keeping an eye on the guest bedroom doors. They both appeared closed, but she could have sworn one moved slightly as she waited for the elevator. When the doors opened, she slipped in and quickly jammed the button to close them again before anyone appeared in the hallway. The last thing she wanted was for Mother to be asking questions about her late night activities.

By the time she returned, Rock was in the shower. She took advantage of the opportunity to change into her pajamas and get into bed while she had the room to herself. Luckily, she'd showered earlier and she made sure to brush her teeth before leaving her place with the litter pan. One thing at a time! Sleeping with Rock was bad enough. Sharing his bathroom went *too far*.

She jumped into bed and pulled the covers to her neck. Rock's claim of sleeping on a cloud rang true as her exhausted body slowly melted into the softest mattress she'd ever encountered. Oh, that felt wonderful. All thoughts ebbed away as she stared at an autographed picture on the wall above the loveseat. The picture featured Rock at a NASCAR race, standing next to a driver in front of his car. After a few moments, she closed her eyes, snuggled a bit, nearly drifting off to sleep when the bathroom door abruptly opened and heavy footsteps padded across the room.

The noise jarred her and she opened her lids a sliver, just enough to catch sight of a magnificent body strolling toward her. Once her brain identified the image, her eyes flew open and she sat up straight, clutching the covers as she tried to suppress a small scream. "You're naked!"

Behind her, Sasha snorted.

"Well, that's how I always take a shower." Rock stood at the foot of the bed with his hands on his hips, wearing nothing but a white towel tied around his narrow waist.

Kim covered her eyes with her hands, trying not to look, but couldn't help sneaking one little peek between her fingers. She had no doubt that he purposely stood there in his birthday suit as a last resort to entice her to sample what he had to offer. No way would she take the bait, but just the same, her heart did an Irish toe dance as she stared between her fingers at a sliver of his wide, bronzed shoulders and sculpted chest. He probably hadn't eaten a Big Mac and super-sized fries in a decade. No man should look that good. At least, no man should look that good tonight!

"Sorry, but this is the way I sleep." He paused, as if waiting for her reaction. When she didn't respond, he pulled back the covers and lifted them high to create a temporary curtain between them, whipped off the towel and crawled into bed, dropping the blankets over his long, sinewy body. With a slow, sexy sigh, he reached up and turned out the lights. The room went inky black.

"Are you sure you don't want my company tonight?"

She pulled the covers up to her neck. "No."

"I swear you won't be disappointed."

"Cut it out. You guaranteed—"

He chuckled and turned away. "I guaranteed I wouldn't make a pass at you again. I didn't guarantee I wouldn't ask again."

"Good night, Rock."

"You'll never know what you missed. Good night, darlin'."

* * *

Kim twisted onto her side and checked the time on the nightstand. The digital clock on the docking station read 3:05 a.m. She sighed and rolled onto her back again, wishing she could get some rest.

"Are you having trouble sleeping?"

She started at the sound of Rock's deep voice permeating the darkness.

"Yeah," she replied, feeling embarrassed, "and I'm sorry if my restlessness is keeping you up. I just can't seem to settle in."

"How long have you been awake?"

"I haven't gone to sleep yet."

She heard a double click and the lamp by his bedside flashed on, flooding the room with soft light. Her eyes blinked furiously, trying to adjust to the change.

Rock lay bare-chested on his back with his hands tucked behind his head, the comforter pushed down to his slim waist. His thick, wavy hair looked tousled from sleeping. A five-o-clock shadow darkened his jaw, but it only added to the sexiness of his pose. She let her imagination wander for a moment and wondered what it would be like to accept his offer and curl up in his arms, nestling her head in the crook of his shoulder, safe and secure...

She suddenly realized by the grin spread across his face that he'd caught her staring and looked away as embarrassment burned her cheeks.

"I sure could use some nice cold water." He reached for the covers. "Would you like some, too?"

Kim shot out of bed. "Yes, but I'll get it! You stay right where you are."

Sasha didn't like her sudden movements and yelped in protest. "Shhhhh," she said as she snatched Sasha off the bed and dropped the dog into the litter box to keep her busy. She stepped into her slippers. "I'll be right back."

"Where are you going?" Rock pointed to an oak cabinet along the wall opposite the bed. "The fridge is over there."

Oh. Right. A bedroom this luxurious should have its own butler, too.

She opened the cabinet door and found a mini-bar, complete with a small refrigerator and a sink. The refrigerator held an assortment of beers, wine and chilled water. After rummaging through the cupboard, she returned to Rock's side of the bed with two crystal tumblers of sparkling water over ice.

Rock accepted a glass as his dark-eyed gaze swept incredulously over her long-sleeved granny gown, thermal leggings and bunny slippers. "What are you wearing?"

"They're called pajamas. Sorry, but this is the way I sleep," she said cocking one eyebrow, "especially when I'm in bed with a guy like you."

"Does that happen often?" He laughed. "You are *so* cute."

"I'm *so* not getting into anything X-rated with you, no matter how many angles you try." Kim scooped up Sasha with her free hand and kicked off her slippers then climbed back into bed, sitting cross-legged on top of the blankets. She put Sasha back on the throw pillow between them. "You should have realized by now that flattery will get you absolutely nowhere with me, mister."

He quickly drained his water and set the glass on his nightstand. "You're a very attractive woman, Kim. I mean that, even though you don't want me to say it. I find your old-fashioned ideals quite refreshing. Nowadays, that's a rare trait in a woman."

She leaned back, resting on her pillow propped against the headboard. "I'm not a prude, if that's what you mean. It's just that... I mean, I just..."

He rolled onto his side, resting his head on the palm of his hand. "Just what?"

She stared into her glass, watching the bubbles surface and wishing the subject had never come up. "It's nothing, really. I'm not here to bore you with my life."

"Hey," he said softly and reached out, lightly twining his fingers through hers, "you're anything but boring to me. What's wrong?"

The touch of his fingers caressing her palm shifted her senses into overdrive, but she purposely avoided looking at his hand lest he interpreted it as encouragement. Instead, she pulled away and looked him straight in the eyes. "I don't trust men like you."

His brows furrowed. "What do you mean, like me? You make me sound like I'm some kind of villain."

Kim sipped her water and stared at the ceiling. "Where should I start? You're rich, you're powerful and your love life is like a revolving door. Once in a while someone gets hurt, but it's never you and when it happens, it doesn't concern you because she has a problem, not you."

"No, you're wrong. That's not me at all." He touched her chin with his finger and turned her face toward him. His eyes narrowed with intensity. "Someone hurt you deeply, didn't he?"

"Yes, but when you're a little girl, any man who takes an interest in you and then abandons you ends up hurting you, even if he didn't mean to."

His face softened with concern, but of course, he didn't understand. No one ever did. Sadly, not even Veronica did when she was alive.

"Tell me what happened." When she shook her head, he stroked her cheek with his thumb and said gently, "Hey, I'm a good listener and since I can't sleep either, I've got all night. Please, tell me what went wrong."

Sasha began to whimper.

"It's too late for that." Kim smiled to cover up her sadness. "The little girl survived and eventually grew up, but—"

"It's never too late to change your mind. Why won't you trust me?"

"I'm sorry, Rock. It's not you. It's—it's me. I can't trust anyone."

He sat up and folded his arms across his chest, mulling over her admission. "What about your father? Why can't you trust him?"

"I don't know him." She glanced away, hating the hollow feeling that gnawed deep inside. "His identity has always been a mystery. Oh, growing up, I asked dozens of questions about him, but my mother refused to talk about her past. Eventually, I accepted the fact that she didn't want me to know and I stopped pestering her." She shifted on the bed, straightening her legs and crossing them at the ankles. "I've always assumed that's why she kept silent."

"How could your father hurt you if you never knew him?"

"He didn't, but his replacement did. Almost all of his replacements did."

Rock lay back against his pillows, silent, waiting for her to continue.

"If you'd known my mother, you'd understand," Kim said. "Veronica stood five-feet-eight-inches in her stocking feet, a glamorous bombshell with luxurious red hair and a show-stopping figure. Back in her day, she had no problem attracting men because she looked so much like Rita Hayworth, she could have passed for a twin sister."

"Rita who?"

"Rita Hayworth," Kim repeated and sipped her water, "a s   , sultry redhead who danced and starred in movies back in the 30s and 40s with the likes of Glenn Ford, Cary Grant and Fred Astaire."

He tweaked a couple strands of her blonde pixie cut. "You must take after your father's side of the family then."

She shrugged. "I guess so. Anyway, Veronica knew the power that her exquisite beauty and sexual charisma gave her over men and she used that influence to snare rich and powerful lovers."

"And you think I'm just like one of her rich and powerful lovers. I see..."

"Actually, you don't see, but I'll explain." Kim held out her hand and offered Sasha a drink from her glass. "Most of the men my mother dated were good to me; some even treated me like a princess. I guess they felt sorry for the shy little girl who spent her life standing in the shadows, all but forgotten. Sometimes I'd get presents or candy. Mostly I'd get money, but what I really wanted money couldn't buy—a daddy to call my own. Every time I thought God had answered my prayers, another relationship would end and I would never hear from that man again. Veronica's possessiveness and self-centeredness drove away every man she ever loved."

Sasha finished lapping water and looked up. Kim pulled the glass away and set it on her nightstand. "She never understood how it affected me. I would go into a depression just as deeply as she did every time we found ourselves alone again. Veronica missed the attention, expensive gifts, limousines and flattery, but I lost the only thing that gave me hope."

"*Hope* is highly overrated, darlin'." Rock stared intently into her eyes. "You don't get anywhere by hoping for anything. You take responsibility for yourself and start over, especially in matters of the heart. There's a saying, 'change your mind, change your life.' It works. I'm living proof. Diona's betrayal hurt more than I care to admit, but I'm leaving the past behind and taking life one day at a time," he said as he reached over and wrapped his fingers around hers, "and you can, too."

Chapter 4

Saturday afternoon, December 19

Christmas spirit decked the halls at the Mall of America in twinkling lights, glittering ornaments and miles of garland strung everywhere as Rock maneuvered Zelda's wheelchair through the shoulder-to-shoulder crowd.

Are we having fun yet?

Never in his life had he witnessed so many stressed out people, waiting in the checkout line to pay, waiting for sales help to discuss an item or waiting for people to simply get out of the way. Disorganized, slow-moving masses always gave him a monster headache and today proved no different. He needed a painkiller before his head exploded, but this circus of a mall housed over five hundred stores and if it did have a drugstore, he'd never find it in a million years. A glass of Chardonnay would have to suffice. That is, if they could get a reservation for dinner.

His phone buzzed in his pocket. He'd deliberately set it on vibrate because he knew that between the nauseating drone of holiday elevator music and the clamor of thousands of people, he'd never hear it, anyway. He stopped Zelda's wheelchair in the sea of milling shoppers, ignoring the flow of people around them and motioned for the nurse to take over as he turned away to answer his phone. "Hey, where are you?"

"I'm in front of the tea shop. I found the sandwiches and the scones your mother wanted." Kim's sweet voice sounded unnaturally tinny against the din. "Where are *you?*"

Darned if I know....

He looked around. "We're on the second level…close to Macy's. Is that in the ballpark of your location?"

"I think so. If you stay put I should be able to catch up with you in a couple minutes." Her reply took on a breathless quality, as though she'd begun to maneuver—or fight—her way to the escalator. "How's your mother holding up?"

"She's shopping up a storm, but she still hasn't found anything for you."

"And that surprises you? Rock, she drummed up that excuse just to get you to bring her here." Kim laughed. "It worked, didn't it?"

He glanced at his mother. Zelda held three large bags on her lap besides her full-length Chinchilla coat and purse. Despite her delicate health, she showed no signs of slowing down. She gestured to him to hurry up as she barked orders to the nurse to wheel her over to the department store.

Marie didn't utter a word. Instead, she smiled coyly at Rock, batting her eyelashes through her oversized eyeglasses while she waited for him to finish his call and rejoin them. She'd been doing that eye thing all day. At first he'd ignored her flirting, considering it harmless and amusing, but through the morning she'd become so friendly that it bordered on annoying.

He pushed the thought aside for now, straining to hear Kim. "What did you say?"

"I said it's odd you mentioned the word *storm.* I just heard that—ouch!" After a short pause and some unintelligible grumbling she said, "Somebody's kid just whacked me with his new light saber. I'd better pay attention to where I'm going. Talk to you soon."

He'd barely put his phone away and walked back to Zelda when

Kim rushed through the crowd, waving.

"My dear," Zelda said, wheeling her chair around, looking festive in her green sweater and slacks, "did you get the reservations for dinner?"

Kim put her hand over her heart to calm her breathing and shook her head. "I'm sorry, Zelda, but the restaurant isn't taking any more customers. The storm has arrived," she said in between breaths. "It just started snowing about fifteen minutes ago, but it's already coming down so hard that visibility is less than a quarter mile. I heard a security guard say the mall is closing early." She turned to Rock. "Perhaps we'd better get going, too."

Zelda looked annoyed and turned to her son. "You've been driving in snow for years. What's a storm now and then? We can't go yet. I still haven't found a wedding present for you."

Kim looked up from her phone and visibly shivered. "According to the Channel 4 weather app, blizzard-like conditions are coming and we could receive at least a foot of snow."

Rock grabbed the wheelchair by the handles and turned toward the nearest exit. Though he hated to disappoint Zelda, her safety mattered more. "I'm sorry, Mother, but we can't delay. It's going to be tough getting home if the roads are slippery."

Kim fell into step beside him. Marie, looking like a blizzard herself in her starched white dress, stockings and shoes, fell into step on his other side—sticking closer than an ace bandage. As they passed an upscale jewelry store, a tall, gray-haired gentleman in a navy wool suit stood at the forefront, pulling a metal curtain across the opening.

"Well, hello," he said in a smooth, but jovial voice and stopped to offer his hand. "Rock Henderson, what brings you out to the mall on a day like this?"

"Harry," Rock replied evenly, nodding as he halted the wheelchair and leaned forward to shake Harry's hand. "Not a thing. I'm just the chauffeur today."

He introduced the women to Harry Silverstone. When Zelda shook his hand, she refused to let go. "My good man, how do you know my son?"

Harry smiled and extracted himself from her grip then placed a hand on Rock's shoulder. "Why, he's one of my best customers and a good friend. We meet for golf nearly every Wednesday in the summer."

"Oh, he is, is he?" She craned her neck to look through the curtain at the sparkling gems displayed in the glass cases. "Then you must be sizing the rings."

Harry's practiced aplomb faltered ever so slightly. He glanced from Rock to Kim to Zelda. "The rings...?"

"That's what I said," Zelda replied in an imperious tone. "If the set is ready, we'll take it now. I'm ill you know," she put her hand over her heart, "and I'd like to see the wedding ring before I leave this world."

Kim suddenly became extremely interested in a loose button on the gold silk blouse she'd picked out of Diona's wardrobe that morning.

Rock put his arm around her and pulled her close, buying time while wondering how to explain his way out of this one. Unfortunately, he couldn't. Harry knew about his tumultuous relationship with Diona and the reason for breaking off their engagement, but he had no idea what Rock was up to now. Rock stared hard at his favorite salesman and friend, hoping Harry would read between the lines and come up with something. Anything.

"Ah, yeah...," Rock said, "you know...the—the wedding rings..."

Harry hesitated for a moment then an odd light flickered in his eyes. "Oh, *those rings*. Of course, the set is ready. I'd planned to give you a call this afternoon. How fortunate of you to stop by." He sounded just a tad too enthusiastic as he pulled back the metal curtain. "Come right in. I'll just be a minute."

Rock pushed Zelda's chair into the store, wondering what Harry had up his sleeve. He stopped at a long glass case where an employee stood pulling out the display boxes to be stored in the vault. That didn't dampen Zelda's spirits, though. She began shopping the moment her gaze fell on the jewels, her eyes sparkling brighter than the gems.

The nurse stood off to one side, however, checking her watch and tapping her foot as though impatient to leave.

Within a minute, Harry reappeared with a small black box. He headed straight for Kim and held it out, displaying a four-carat diamond.

"Here you are, Mrs. Henderson. Your princess cut solitaire set is going to look so beautiful on your hand, but I'll give Rock the pleasure of performing that little duty." Harry flashed a megawatt smile and handed the box to Rock.

He had no choice now but to follow through with this little charade.

Kim's eyes grew wide as her gaze fell on the exquisite wedding set. Everyone moved in close to watch Rock carefully remove it from the box and place it on her finger. Somehow, this little scene seemed too real for comfort. He'd been through this ritual before and never felt a thing, but this time a fine sheen of perspiration formed on his upper lip. He hoped no one would notice his nervousness as he took the solitaire, paired with a plain wedding band and slipped it on her finger.

The solitaire went on easily and looked stunning, as though the jeweler had custom made it just for her. Kim held her hand out, her wide blue eyes shining as she stared with fascination at the shimmering diamond. She looked up; their gazes met. When she smiled, the protective wall around the core of his heart began to soften. She didn't fit his image of a perfect woman, she'd said so herself, but perhaps he'd been ascribing to the wrong image all along. Maybe someday he would find a woman he could trust—perhaps someone like her, who would promise to have and to hold forever, in sickness and in health and not divulge corporate secrets. A simple thought startled him. Maybe he already had...

"There you are, Mrs. Henderson," Harry said smoothly. "It's a perfect fit—a beautiful diamond for a beautiful woman."

Rock cleared his throat. "Refresh my memory, Harry. We never got around to dealing on the price. How much did this chunk of ice set me back?"

"Rock, Rock," Harry implored, raising his hands in protest, "don't spoil the moment."

"Harry..."

The jeweler let out a deep sigh and shook his head. "You always drive such a hard bargain with me, Rock, so I'm willing to give you a deal. I'll let it go for forty-five thousand."

What!? They'd played practical jokes on each other in the past, but this time Rock didn't find the gag very funny.

Harry rested his hand on Rock's shoulder again, giving it a fatherly squeeze. "Don't worry about it; I put it on your account. Take your bride home before the snowstorm forces you all to get a room here. We'll finalize the terms later."

Rock blinked, wondering if he'd heard right. How had things gotten so out of control? One little white lie had led to another and now he not only had a wife, but a jewelry bill the size of Rhode Island. What else would he be expected to produce—grandchildren?

* * *

Two hours later, they finally arrived home, tired, hungry and stressed out from the treacherous conditions.

"That's the first time it has ever taken me two hours to make a twenty minute drive," Rock said wearily as he took his mother's fur

48

coat and hung it in the foyer closet. "I couldn't believe all the cars we passed stuck in the ditch. I'm glad we didn't end up like that."

"You're a good driver." Kim handed him her coat to put away. Her new wedding rings sparkled under the foyer chandelier, making her conscious of them on her hand. "Thank you for bringing us home safely."

"I'm hungry," Zelda complained loudly. "What are we going to do for dinner? You mentioned earlier that your servant is on holiday this week. I don't suppose we could find someone to deliver takeaway in this weather."

Kim took Zelda's hat and gloves and set them in the closet on the shelf. "I could make dinner." She turned around to find everyone staring at her. "What, did I say something wrong?"

Zelda signaled Marie to push her into the living room. "My son has servants to do such things. What would you, the daughter of a wealthy businessman, know about domestic duties?"

Kim cast a questioning look at Rock, wondering what to say now. His furrowed brows reminded her they were talking about Diona Daye, a wealthy, spoiled socialite who probably didn't know a rolling pin from a paint roller, not Kim Stratton, a middle-class working girl.

"Well," she said casually and forced a laugh, "it's a hobby of mine. I love to dabble in the kitchen when Rock is at the office and our housekeeper has the day off. My specialty is organic foods."

Zelda responded with a wry smirk as Marie wheeled her down the hallway. "What do you cook, seeds and twigs?"

Kim put on her best smile and silently counted to ten. Boy, this week had better go fast. "Whatever Rock is hungry for, whether it's as simple as roast and potatoes or something more interesting, like Italian. He likes everything I make."

Rock hooked his arm around hers as they fell in behind. "Italian sounds wonderful, darlin'. I haven't had anything to eat since breakfast.

But, you'd better check to see if I—we have any food."

"We have plenty of food," Kim said, assuming that Rock probably had no idea what groceries his housekeeper had stocked in his kitchen. She silently pointed downward, indicating that she meant to get additional food from her condominium on the sixth floor. "I'll poke around in the freezer and check the pantry in our storage locker in the basement to see what we have. I'm sure I can rustle up the ingredients for chicken picatta or lasagna. Which would you like? Chicken picatta is probably healthier."

Zelda spun her wheelchair around at the doorway to the living room. "What's wrong with lasagna?"

Rock stopped abruptly behind her. "Mother, are you sure you should eat that? Given your medical issues, aren't you on a special diet?"

Zelda gave him a stern look. "I'll make an exception tonight. Since we're going to be cooped up in this attic until it quits snowing, we must all make sacrifices."

She turned and motioned to Marie to roll her chair into the living room, leaving Rock and Kim to stare after her.

"*Hoo-kay,*" Kim said to no one in particular. "Lasagna it is then. I use all natural ingredients and..."

Her mouth fell open in shock. The living room, strewn with shredded newspaper, looked like a tornado disaster area. Someone or something had clawed the bottom of one of the ice blue drapes to pieces. An overturned flowerpot lay on the carpet, the dirt spread indiscriminately across the room.

"What in the world happened to this place?"

Marie tiptoed around the furniture and collapsed into an easy chair. Folding her legs under her, she looked like she planned to stay there until further notice.

Rock squeezed past Zelda's wheelchair and stood off to one side so as not to walk in the potting soil. He gripped his hands on his hips and surveyed the carnage with disgust. "It looks to me like something on four legs went berserk." He pointed at the damaged curtain. "Something equipped with sharp claws and an evil mind."

Kim looked around, alarmed. "Where is Sasha?"

A whimpering sound, coming from behind the sofa, answered to her voice. She knelt down and patted a clean spot on the rug. "Here, Sasha, come on, girl. Come out, you're safe now."

Two liquid eyes set in a white mask with a tiny snout soon emerged. The dog canvassed the room for danger then darted out, making a beeline for the safety of Kim's arms. She scooped up her baby and kissed her on the head. "You're shaking. What happened while we were gone?"

Sasha didn't answer. She just looked up at Kim with sorrowful eyes.

"Roscoe, where are you?" Zelda bellowed. The tabby emerged at the sound of her voice, trotted across the room with a loud meow and jumped into her lap. "My poor frightened pussy cat." She stoked his arched back. "Look what that naughty little dog did."

Kim turned around and went back into the hallway before she said something she knew she'd regret.

"I'll put Sasha in a safe place then get the vacuum and clean up the mess," she said to Rock as she headed toward his bedroom. "I'm not sure how much will come out of the carpet, but it's not ground in so the vacuum should get most of it. We'll probably have to get it steam cleaned after Christmas."

On the way to Rock's bedroom, she found a trail of white along the floor. It looked like shredded toilet paper. Curious, she ducked into the bath situated between two bedrooms and found a mountain of the stuff on the floor. Boy, that cat must have had a blast.

It didn't take her long to find the vacuum and get started putting the place back in order. Rock picked up as much of the newspaper pieces as he could while she vacuumed the crumbles of black dirt. Marie didn't bother to help, but at least she stayed out of the way. Once cleaned, the carpet looked almost as good as before the incident, but a couple of black spots refused to come out. The drapes were a total loss.

Rock migrated into the family room, an adjoining area with huge corner windows and a full-service bar, and put a movie into the DVD player to entertain everyone while Kim took the elevator to the "storage area," secretly known as the condo at 601E.

*   *   *

Once in the solitude of her apartment, she collapsed onto one of the loveseats and exhaled her first relaxed breath since nine o'clock last night. She and Rock had spent a good part of the night talking, but strangely, she didn't feel tired. She had no doubt that would change, though, if they didn't get some sleep tonight!

Someone had taped a flyer to her door, reminding her of the building association's annual holiday potluck get-together in the main party room at six o'clock that evening on the first floor. The residents put on a fantastic buffet every year of appetizers, entrees and just about every dessert a person could imagine. She'd looked forward to it and had intended to bring the lasagna, homemade garlic bread and a dessert, but that plan fell apart last night when Rock showed up at the door. Now it seemed important to stay out of sight to avoid questions about him, not to mention the gossip that would mutate into gospel if anyone found out they were cohabitating for a week. Deep down, she wished she could bring him as her guest. It would be such fun to be his date at a party, but she knew it would never happen. Once this week ended, so did their relationship. They were doing each other a favor and nothing more.

Grabbing a wicker clothesbasket, she mentally ticked off the ingredients in her head as she filled it with groceries. Once she had everything packed, she cast a last look around the kitchen to make sure she hadn't forgotten anything and as an afterthought, grabbed a couple Christmas decorations that would look nice on the table. Now to lug this basket downstairs and back into Rock's elevator before anyone saw her...

*　　*　　*

The bold aroma of Darjeeling tea filled her nostrils as Kim stepped off the elevator and walked through the penthouse foyer. "I'm b-a-a-c-k," she called out. "Anyone want to give me a hand with these groceries?" No one answered.

In the family room, she found Zelda reclining on a Lazy Boy, watching *The Sorcerer's Stone* on Rock's wide-screen TV and indulging in an afternoon 'cuppa' of tea with a small array of the finger-length sandwiches and scones that Kim had purchased at the mall. Marie, on the other hand, had taken a spot on the sofa next to Rock and sat so close to him that if she moved another inch or two, she'd be in his lap.

What's wrong with the woman, anyway? Why was this dippy nurse coming on to her husband? The thought suddenly startled her.

When did I start thinking of Rock as my husband?

She turned away so no one could see her confusion and swiftly walked back to the kitchen. Once out of sight, she examined her hand. The ring sparkled like a star on a clear night. It would be so easy to fall in love with it, but it represented a lie and she planned to give it back to Rock as soon as Zelda left for home.

"Time to get to work," she said aloud and started pulling open cabinet doors to find the utensils she needed. "This meal isn't going to prepare itself."

She figured out how to set the oven temperature then pulled out an oblong pan for the lasagna and began chopping onions to add to the browning meat. After a few minutes she became so engrossed in her work, she didn't hear anyone come into the kitchen.

"Need any help?"

Rock's voice surprised her and she whirled around so fast the knife almost flew out of her hand. "Oh," she said placing one palm across her heart, "you scared me."

"I'm sorry," he said softly, the corners of his chocolate eyes crinkling as he smiled. "I just came to see if you could use a helper."

"Really?" She couldn't help smiling back. He sure didn't look like a cook's helper in his tight, low-rise jeans and navy V-neck sweater. More like the cover model of a magazine. She made a conscious effort to tear her gaze away from his tall, muscled frame then grabbed a bag of spinach and a colander. "Here, rinse this and put it in the wooden bowl next to the sink filled with strips of red and green peppers. The utensils are lying next to it. Mix it up well and put it in the refrigerator to chill. Just before we sit down for dinner, you can put it on the dining room table next to the oil and vinegar cruets."

She handed him a bottle of liquid soap to wash his hands. "What's the matter, did you get tired of watching Harry Potter?"

Rock turned on the water and lathered up. "No, I got annoyed with a certain clinging vine on the couch." He dabbed a goatee of white bubbles on her chin. "I'd rather be in here with you any day. Besides, I want to see if you really can cook."

She turned back to the stove before he could see her beaming with pride. "You'll see."

For the next half hour, they worked side-by-side, putting together the evening meal. Once the lasagna went into the oven, they set the timer and began decorating the dining room. Kim spread a red plaid tablecloth on the table and a small, but elegant basket for a centerpiece made of pine boughs, apples and pinecones. Red ribbons tied into bows garnished each end of the handle. Next, they set the table with china, silverware and crystal. A little while later she approached the table to add a set of red candles when suddenly her feet slipped out from under her and she landed on her backside on the oak floor.

"What the..." Rock exclaimed as he rushed into the dining room and found her sprawled on her back. "Are you all right?" He threw down his dishtowel and took her hands, gazing upon her with tenderness and concern. "What happened?"

"I don't know..." Dazed, Kim looked around as he helped her to feet. "One moment I was walking upright, then before I knew what happened I'd crashed and burned."

He knelt and ran his fingers across a shiny spot on the wood. "There's oil on the floor. You must have spilled some when you put the cruets on the table."

"No." Kim shook her head. "Not a drop leaked from either bottle. Look at them. The stoppers are on tight."

He stood up. "That's strange. Well, I'll get a towel and some soap and clean it off. Do you feel well enough to finish dinner? If not, you can tell me what to do and I'll take care of it."

Wow. What a sweetie. She waved away the question as she limped backed into the kitchen, determined to finish what she started.

"I'm fine, just a little shook up, that's all, but thank you for asking. I'll start making the garlic bread right away. The lasagna is coming out of the oven in a couple minutes."

Rock inhaled a deep breath. "Hmm, that smells good." He rubbed his taught stomach. "I'm definitely looking forward to this."

*   *   *

Rock dimmed the chandelier and lit the candles as they took their places at the table. Kim took the seat next to Rock. Marie pulled away a chair and positioned Zelda's wheelchair at the end of the table, saving the other place next to Rock for herself.

"Rock, dear, give the blessing, please," Zelda insisted and folded her hands while Marie set the brake on her wheelchair. Kim bowed her head, but a heavy thud caught her attention and she opened her eyes in time to see two furry paws land on her Lennox china plate. Annoyed, she looked up and received a fat, furry belly in her face. Obviously, Roscoe wanted to join the fun, too. Unfortunately, no one had invited him. He yowled in protest when Rock grabbed him and set him on the floor.

The meal started out pleasant with light conversation as they passed around the spinach salad. During the meal, Kim said little, nervously nibbling on her food while she observed everyone's reaction to her cooking.

Rock took great delight in dishing up the main course, smiling as he filled plates with lasagna for everyone then helped himself to a double portion. He spoke only when spoken to, preferring to substitute filling his stomach for conversation. Kim watched him devour his pasta and garlic toast with such gusto she wondered when he'd last had a home cooked meal. A real home cooked meal made from scratch with organic ingredients, not that home-ready stuff filled with salt and preservatives sold in the grocery store.

Marie had ignored her salad and now sat listlessly picking at her entree. She frowned at her plate, refusing to look up. Something about her bothered Kim. Her attitude and behavior just didn't jive with her job description. Her oversized glasses were homely and too large for her face. The drab, mousey chignon fastened at the back of her head appeared a bit skewed. A small coppery tendril escaped from the bun, looking oddly out of place.

That's strange, Kim thought to herself. *It doesn't match the rest of her hair.*

"Everything is delicious," Zelda announced as she reached across the table and helped herself to a second square of lasagna. "Where did you learn to cook like this?"

"I taught myself through trial and error." Kim patted her lips with her napkin. "As a kid, I'd watch all those cooking shows on television and over the years the idea stuck with me. The chefs always made everything look so easy." She laughed. "I've made my share of mistakes, but little by little, I've come to master the art of following a recipe."

"What about your mother?" Zelda picked through the basket of garlic toast. "Did she cook as well?"

Kim grasped her water glass, but stopped just short of taking a sip. "Veronica couldn't boil water, as the saying goes. She preferred her meals prepared and served by someone else, preferably in a waiter's uniform."

"My goodness," Zelda said, "for a woman born into wealth, you're quite the anomaly. You can cook and you can clean, but do you have what it takes to make my son happy?"

Rock stopped eating, his fork frozen in front of his mouth. "That was uncalled for, Mother."

Marie took a sip of water and began chewing loudly on a chunk of ice.

"I'd say it's quite appropriate." She glared at him with a challenging lift to her chin. "I want to die with the assurance that you've made a good match. Your wife needs to be more than a live-in servant. You need a woman who is your equal in every way."

Rock put down his forkful of lasagna and shook his head, as though he found the question ridiculous. "She *is* my equal in every way." Reaching out, he covered Kim's hand with his broad palm and curled his fingers around hers, though his dark eyes studied her with serious intent. "I admire her loyalty and selfless dedication to others. It's a refreshing change from the vain, self-centered women I used to date. She's perfect just the way she is."

Kim blinked; taken aback that he'd just quoted her own previous comment back to her. Did he actually mean that? Probably not. He was just holding his own against Zelda.

She didn't have time to ponder it, though, because Marie suddenly burst into a coughing spasm, apparently choking on the ice in her mouth.

Purple-faced, Marie shoved her chair away from the table and stomped out of the room. Kim jumped up and went after her. Rock followed close behind.

"Are you all right?" Kim cried as she rushed into the living room, ready to apply the Heimlich maneuver if need be. She didn't know if the woman understood her words, but undoubtedly, her tone of voice conveyed her concern.

Marie stopped and whirled around, glaring as though Kim had overstepped her bounds by questioning a nurse about her condition. Rock repeated the question, but when he spoke, she defiantly turned and walked away, heading into the hallway toward her bedroom.

Confused, Kim raised her palms. "What did I say that offended her so much?"

Rock stared at the wide doorway leading to the hall. "I have no idea. Maybe it upset her to hear me arguing with Mother."

"She'll come around," Zelda announced, rolling her chair into the living room next to Kim. "My dear, I'll take my coffee in here. Rock, turn on the fireplace and then bring me a blanket."

Kim held Zelda's wheelchair in place then helped the woman move to a comfortable seat on the sofa. Zelda sat back and sighed, making no effort to conceal how much she hated being dependent upon others.

"You get the blanket, Rock. I'll get dessert," Kim said as she pushed the wheelchair out of the way. "Meet you back here in five."

True to her word, within five minutes Kim reappeared with a tray of hand-made spumoni covered in warm brandy sauce and a carafe of fresh ground decaf. Rock and Zelda sat on the sofa, smiling as she served dessert. Marie failed to show.

Zelda enjoyed a spoonful of ice cream, or a delicious sweet, as she called it, her gaze critically sweeping the living room. "Where's the Christmas tree?" She looked directly at Kim. "From the barren look of this place, one would think you'd just moved in."

Kim glanced around quickly, as though seeing the space for the first time. It could, perhaps, use a flocked tree in front of the windows, some bayberry candles, fresh pine garland and table runners to enhance the room's beautiful furnishings, but she'd been so busy trying to get along with her make-believe monster-in-law and that cranky nurse-for-the-worse that she'd never noticed Rock hadn't bothered to decorate his house for Christmas.

"You're right," she confessed and poured herself a cup of the rich, aromatic coffee. "We've both been too busy. Rock has to devote his time to clients and because it's the holiday season, I've been spending extra hours at the crisis nursery to give the staff some needed time off."

Zelda looked surprised. "So, you do volunteer work at a nursery?"

"Yes, it's actually a shelter for small children who are at risk for neglect and abuse." She didn't need to worry about sounding convincing this time because it was the truth. "Since we're snowed in anyway," she added, changing the subject, "we might as well put up our tree tomorrow. Right, Rock?"

Rock gave her a confused look as he set his empty bowl on the coffee table. "Where are we going to get a tree?"

Kim shot him an annoyed glare. Men could be so clueless sometimes! "From the *storage locker*, remember? The same place we store the extra food. We'll go downstairs tomorrow, after breakfast, and gather up everything we need."

Rock wrapped his long fingers around a china coffee mug and

relaxed in his chair by the fire, his eyes twinkling at her code for raiding the condo. "Whatever you say, darlin'."

Chapter 5

"I have to run down to Mrs. Doyle's unit on the second floor," Kim announced later that night as she stood in Rock's walk-in closet and selected a gold cashmere sweater to match her blouse from the real Diona's wardrobe.

"Oh? What's the matter?" He'd asked the question politely, but she sensed his disappointment that she planned to leave.

She appeared in the closet doorway with the sweater, jamming her arms through the sleeves. "Mrs. Doyle just called my cell phone and said she needs help changing her colostomy bag. The poor woman has arthritis in her hands and tends to drop things."

Kim began hastily buttoning the front of her sweater as she searched the room for her purse. "She probably had a glass of Mogen David at the association party tonight and now she's afraid of having an accident. I don't mind helping her out now and then. We've been friends since I moved in. Who knows, I might get some good gossip about the upcoming vote out of the deal."

She found her purse and rummaged through it, looking for her key card. Locating it, she shoved the card in the pocket of her slacks and tossed the purse on the bed. "I have to stop at my place to get some latex gloves first so that will take extra time, but I won't be gone long. Keep an eye on Sasha for me, okay? Be back in a little while."

Kim hurried into the hallway, her flats padding quietly on the

61

marble floor. She reached the elevator in the foyer and pressed the button, wondering who might be at the party or simply milling around the lobby this time of night, chatting with friends. Though she wanted to drop into the party room and sample a few of her favorite foods, she didn't have time to visit with neighbors and certainly didn't want to talk about her activities for the week. Besides, if she stayed away too long, Zelda might get suspicious.

Speak of the devil, Zelda's door suddenly opened. She peered out wearing a black velour sweat suit and a thick white sweater, something hand-knitted with a reindeer design. "Going somewhere?"

Oh-oh, busted...

Kim stopped and looked past her shoulder. "I'm going to visit a neighbor."

Zelda responded with a disapproving frown. "Isn't it a bit late for socializing?"

Kim pressed the elevator button again, anxious to escape Mother Goose's scrutiny. "It isn't exactly a social call. Mrs. Doyle is elderly and has medical issues. She sometimes needs assistance."

"Will you be gone long?"

"About an hour or so."

Zelda looked annoyed, as though Kim's leaving inconvenienced her.

"Are you feeling all right?" She stared at Zelda's sweater, wondering why the woman needed extra warmth. "I hope you're not getting a chill."

"Of course not," Zelda snapped, sounding a bit defensive. "I'm just trying it on to see if it matches my suit."

Whatever.

The elevator softly chimed. Kim turned and watched the doors silently glide open, grateful to escape. She dealt with difficult situations on a regular basis, but Zelda's imperious personality increasingly grated on her. No way could she handle this woman for much longer. Unfortunately, she needed to hang on for Rock's sake. Forcing herself to smile, she woodenly waved goodbye as the elevator doors closed then breathed a sigh of relief over managing to dodge the old bat's scrutiny. For now, anyway.

*　　*　　*

Steady footfalls whispered a soft echo in her wake as Kim ventured through the dark foyer, carrying a shrink-wrapped china plate heaped with bars, cookies and sweet breads from the party. Mrs. Doyle had insisted she help herself to a sampling of the desserts that residents had delivered as neighborly Christmas gifts to the elderly lady's apartment. Since Kim hadn't had time to bake anything herself, she figured the goodies would make a nice surprise for Rock and his guests.

She slowed down and began to tiptoe as she passed Zelda's bedroom. A sliver of light knifed through the one-inch space of Zelda's partially-opened door, casting a spear of golden radiance across the black marble floor. The door didn't move, but she sensed Zelda watching her as she made her way to Rock's bedroom. Not wanting to give the old lady cause to start up another conversation, she kept on walking, pretending she hadn't suspected anything.

Instead of going straight to Rock's room, however, she made a last minute decision to put the goodies on the bar in the family room and pick up some sparkling water at the same time. On her way through the doorway, she stopped, recoiling at the acrid smell of cigarettes near the sliding door. The Robertsons were obviously out on their balcony smoking again...in the dark...in the snowstorm. Gee, didn't they ever take a break?

She approached the bar and found a wine key lying next to a ring of liquid on the black and silver granite countertop. Rock must have opened a bottle of wine to have a glass at bedtime. Too tired to clean up the spot, she placed the treats on the counter, checked the refrigerator then left the room.

As she entered the bedroom, Rock emerged from the bathroom, wearing a pair of navy and green plaid pajama bottoms, sporting the brand 'Joe Boxer' on the elastic waistband. The pajamas hung low on his hips, accentuating his long torso and legs. She tried not to stare, but those hip-hugging pants and his sinewy bare chest looked sexier and more masculine to her than his little episode last night strutting around in nothing but his birthday suit garnished with a towel.

How sweet, she thought, that he'd decided to be a good boy and wear clothes to bed.

"There isn't any sparkling water in the family room," Kim said seriously, trying to resist focusing on the dusting of black hair sprinkled across his broad chest. "I guess we'll have to get some tomorrow. That is, if we get plowed out."

He walked over to the mini-bar, leaving a vapor trail of musky cologne in his wake. "There's plenty in here." He opened the refrigerator. "Would you like a glass after you take a shower?"

"I could use some right now."

Sasha crawled out from under the bed and whined. Kim picked up the dog and set her on one of the pillows piled in the center of the mattress. "I stopped in at my place and took a shower." She opened a dresser drawer and pulled out her pajamas. "I'll be right back."

When she emerged from the bathroom wearing her nightgown, Rock had prepared for her a crystal tumbler filled with ice, water and a generous wedge of lime. He grinned as his gaze swept her from head to toe. "What, no leggings tonight?"

She set the glass on the nightstand before crawling onto the bed. "They made me too warm last night. I think that's why I couldn't sleep."

"Are you sure the extra clothes had something to do with it?" He flashed a killer smile and placed his hands on his hips. "Maybe you've got the hots for me and you just don't want to admit it."

Kim tried to fake an annoyed look, but his sudden comeback made her burst out laughing instead. At the same time, a gulp of sparkling water shot back up her throat like Old Faithful, cutting off her air and causing her to cough violently.

"Taking lessons from the nurse?" he teased in a light-hearted tone as he patted her on the back. "Keep this up and you're going to get mouth-to-mouth resuscitation."

"Don't you dare," she managed to croak out between coughs. "I'm just fine." She scooted under the covers and with a satisfied sigh, sunk her cheek into the feather-soft pillow. "Except for one thing; I'm so tired I could sleep through an earthquake."

*   *   *

An hour later, Rock activated the light on his side of the bed and threw back the covers. He swung his legs over the side of the bed and sat up, rubbing his eyes with the heels of his hands. "I can't sleep."

This time he knew why. He couldn't get Kim off his mind. Spending time with her, eating meals with her, sleeping next to her, or rather, trying to sleep when lying next to her, kept her in his thoughts constantly. How could he not be attracted to such a sweetheart? The more he dwelled on her, the more he realized what an extraordinary woman she'd turned out to be in ways that had never mattered to him in the past. Why hadn't he discovered these qualities in women before? The answer probably stemmed from the fact that he'd always been attracted to the wrong type of woman—the 'vain, self-centered type' as Kim once described it. He'd always been attracted to a certain kind of beauty, but that didn't guarantee a 'good match,' a term his British-born mother used to describe finding the right wife. Women who wore quality on the outside didn't necessarily wear it on the inside where it truly counted. He'd learned that the hard way, but he'd also learned that he had no clue as to how to get close to Kim. She didn't buy into his material status or even his sex appeal. She saw him only as a carbon copy of the numerous lovers who'd drifted in and out of her mother's life. What would it take to convince her that he didn't fit the mold she'd unjustifiably cast for him?

He glanced over his shoulder and saw her staring wide-eyed at the ceiling. The Sausage lay curled up next to her head. "It's awfully dry in here. Are you thirsty?"

She yawned and nodded, raising her hand to cover her mouth. The four-carat diamond on her left hand sparkled like a thousand points of light. Funny, but he'd never noticed the engagement ring on Diona's hand after he had given it to her.

A couple minutes later, he presented Kim with a chilled glass of water spiked with a wedge of lime.

She sat up and kicked off the covers, crossing her feet at the ankles. Her toenails, polished in a sparkly gold color, had red poinsettia leaves hand-painted on them. "What, no wine?"

He stood there holding the glass, trying to figure her out. "I thought you wanted water at night. That's why I stocked the mini-bar with it today."

"I do. Thank you very much," she said with a smile and accepted the glass as she relaxed against her pillows. "Since neither of us can sleep again, I figured maybe you had decided we needed something a little stronger. Isn't that why you opened a bottle in the family room? I saw the wine key lying on the bar."

He frowned as he settled on his side of the bed, contemplating what it would feel like to kiss her cute little toes as he massaged her feet. "I didn't open any wine bottle tonight."

"Hmmm... That's strange," she replied with a suspicious note in her voice. "I wonder if Nurse Ratchet is a closet alcoholic."

"I don't know about that, but she's got great legs," he said without thinking. As soon as the words left his lips, he regretted it immensely. "I-I only meant that she looks too perfect to be a nurse."

Kim merely rolled her eyes.

"Sorry, I meant no offense to you or your profession!" He raised one palm to gesture a truce. "What I mean to say is that she doesn't seem natural in that—"

"In that ridiculous white uniform with matching nylons," Kim stated, finishing the sentence for him. "You're right. No one wears a white shirtwaist dress like that anymore, not in Minnesota, anyway. It's too impractical. She looks like she's on her way to a Halloween party, if you ask me. I'm not sure what her game is, but I'll tell you one thing; she's not a nurse. I've never seen her do anything to care for your mother other than push Zelda's wheelchair around."

Rock adjusted the pillows behind him and sat back. "Come to think of it, I haven't either, but I'm sure Zelda is well aware of the situation and has her reasons for employing the woman." He stared across the room, focusing on Zelda's framed photo on his dresser. "In any case, I hate seeing my mother confined to that rolling jail cell. It's extremely difficult for her to be so dependent upon others, but she has no choice now."

"Zelda is a strong woman," Kim said softly. "You must get your skill for business from her."

He sighed. "You're probably right about that. I sure didn't get it from my dad. Don't get me wrong. I loved him with all my heart, but he never did much to prepare me for adulthood."

"Why, did his business interests take up a lot of time? What profession did he hold?"

"Nothing, at least that I know of."

She looked startled by his blatant admission. "Are you serious?"

"Your family tree isn't the only one with a few sagging limbs." He set down his glass and folded his arms across his chest, deciding to level with her. "In other words, my parents didn't exactly have a fairytale marriage. Dad married Mother for her money. She snagged a

67

dashing American for permanent residency in the United States and freedom from her controlling father. Oh, my parents did love each other in their own way, but they fought about money all the time." He laughed ruefully. "That's putting it mildly, actually. The money came from Mother's trust and she's always kept tight control of it."

The Sausage left her spot on the throw pillow and crawled onto Kim's lap. Rock watched as Kim reached down and gently stroked the dog's back, looking content as she reposed against her pillows. For a moment, he gave into his imagination as a growing desire tempted him to lean over the pillows and kiss her plump lips, letting nature take its course from there...

"So, then how did your dad spend his time?"

To get his mind off Kim's cute, kissable mouth, Rock extended his hand toward the clingy little mutt instead, allowing it to sniff his fingers. He paused, waiting to see if The Sausage would bite him or allow him to pet her. She merely stared at him, resting happily on Kim's lap. After a few moments, he pulled his hand away, relieved that he still had all of his digits, but not ready to press his luck.

"He did what every rich, idle American of his generation did to pass the years. He played golf, arranged card games and drank Scotch with his cronies at the country club." Then, expelling a sigh, Rock said, "And he died at the age of sixty-three."

"Do you miss him?"

"I think about him every day," Rock said sadly and winced, wondering if the pain of losing his father would ever fade. "I miss talking to him most of all. Granted, we didn't have a lot in common, but he really cared about me. Unfortunately, he died before my company started to gain some serious momentum. He didn't live long enough to see the success of my ideas. Dad typically didn't put his feelings into words, but I knew he was very proud of me. He always listened, never judged."

"And Zelda?"

"Ah, Mother means well, but she has an opinion on everything. She likes to be in charge, you know."

Kim gave him a knowing smile. "I gather you've never asked her for financial assistance."

"Not a dime," he stated proudly. "I built my company the old-fashioned way, pay-as-you-go and what I couldn't pay for, I financed on my own. It's been a long, rocky road, but I don't regret any of it." He sighed again. "Except getting tangled up with Diona, of course."

She looked up, pondering his statement with an innocent, blue-eyed gaze, completely unaware of how sexy she looked to him languidly resting against her pillows. For a moment, he imagined himself pulling away the physical barrier between them and kissing her luscious lips...

"I'm so sorry, Rock. I can't understand how she could betray you like that."

His thoughts took a U-turn at the mention of his ex-fiancé-turned-enemy. "She never expected me to find out and I wouldn't have until the damage had been done if I hadn't noticed an email coming through on her phone when she went to take a shower. It's not my way to violate someone else's privacy, but I had to look when I saw the subject line said, "Read and Destroy." It didn't take me long to get a private investigator involved and confirm it with solid proof."

She set the dog between them. "I hope the theft didn't cost you a lot of money."

He absently set his hand on the bed next to The Sausage, palm side down and amazingly, the furry hotdog-on-legs began to lick his fingers.

"Frankly, the issue isn't so much what she stole, but whom she stole it *for* that burned me and ruined my belief in true love. She stole it for her father, the same man who helped me get into business and served as my mentor for years. When my company began growing faster than his, he became jealous and convinced Diona to spy for him. She and I had already been dating for a few months and by that time, I trusted her completely—not only with my heart, but with confidential information, too. Not long after she began coaxing information out of me, we became engaged.

"When a person agrees to take a wedding vow, it's until death do you part, not until a better offer comes along. At least, that's the way it is in my book."

Kim nodded in agreement. "Are you going to prosecute her?"

He lifted his finger and began gently to rub under the dog's chin. "I should, but no. I don't want to hurt her the way she hurt me by getting revenge. I just don't want anything to do with her ever again."

Chapter 6

Sunday morning, December 20

"If I'd known the weather could get this bad in Minnesota, I would have stayed home," Zelda grumbled and stared glumly out the dining room window. "I suppose this bloody storm will keep us from going back to the Mall of America today."

Everyone sat around the oval dining table, drinking coffee while gazing out the windows at the snow-covered parkland along the east bank of the Mississippi Riverfront. Kim cut a glance at Rock and wondered if *he* wished Zelda had stayed home, too, but if he did, he didn't let on. Rock seemed preoccupied as he reclined in his chair with one arm resting on the table, holding his cup of espresso and watching the snow steadily falling. Shadows under his dark eyes hinted at the fatigue setting in from two sleepless nights.

Well, she didn't feel so great herself. They'd talked for more than an hour last night then watched a movie before falling asleep in the wee hours of the morning. All the while they spoke, however, she couldn't shake the feeling that he had something pressing he wanted to say to her. Was he having second thoughts about deceiving his mother? Or did he just want her to invite him to her side of the bed?

She rubbed the back of her aching neck, feeling the heavy toll of going without sleep. If she didn't get some rest soon, she feared she couldn't keep going. Luckily, the storm forced them to stay indoors and provided the perfect excuse to take a mid-day nap. She wondered if she could sneak away for a few hours to hibernate in her own home, where the atmosphere didn't contain guests wearing out their welcome or a certain sexy, dark-haired man.

A gust of wind swirled the snow into a blizzard-like cloud, cutting off their view. About a foot had fallen already, burying everything on the patio under a frozen mountain of white. The local weatherman on the morning newscast had reported that the storm kept rotating in a slow-moving circle, dumping snow and creating wind that caused drifting across open spaces.

Marie shivered, clutching her cup of latte with both hands, courtesy of Rock's fancy coffeemaker in the kitchen and Kim's ability to figure out the contraption. Marie's oversized tortoiseshell glasses looked like twin windows balancing on her slim nose.

Kim broke the gloomy silence by announcing the exciting agenda for the day. "What time do you want to go downstairs and get the tree?"

"What time is dinner?" Zelda interjected before Rock could work up the energy to speak.

Kim focused on Rock to avoid showing her irritation at Miss Crabby Pants for interrupting. "If it's all right with everyone, how about having dinner at around four?" Oh well, never mind sneaking away to take a much-needed siesta. As soon as they finished putting up the tree and decorating the living room, it would be time to start cooking. At least she'd be cleaning up the dishes earlier, though.

He shrugged, seemingly uninterested in food. His hand slowly lifted the espresso cup to his lips and he sipped the steaming liquid, oblivious to Zelda's mood. Kim had never seen him look so tired, but neither had she seen him look so handsome, either. His unshaven jaw and thick black hair, still tousled from sleeping in his luxurious bed, gave him a rugged, masculine look. He turned his head and cleared his throat, as if suddenly realizing she'd spoken to him.

"Four o'clock sounds fine. We're not going out in this weather, anyway. We might as well dine early and watch a movie tonight. Besides, I need to get to bed at a decent hour. It's back to work for me tomorrow and I have to go in early to prepare for a staff meeting at eight o'clock sharp."

"I'm bored with the telly," Zelda announced with a dissatisfied groan. "Let's play cards or put together a puzzle or something." She gave Kim a grouchy look. "What's on the menu tonight?"

Good question, Kim thought and mentally ran through the list of what she had stocked in her kitchen. She definitely needed to go grocery shopping tomorrow once the blizzard stopped and Minneapolis Public Works plowed the streets so she could get out. "Um, would you like meatloaf and mashed potatoes?"

Rock and Zelda stared at each other then suddenly, together, they said, "cottage pie."

Zelda gave an agreeable nod and held up her cup for more coffee. Kim leaned across the table to fill Zelda's cup, not understanding what they meant by cottage pie, but didn't want to appear ignorant so she didn't ask. She figured it must be a British dish of some sort and made a mental note to research it on the Internet when time permitted. If Rock liked that dish, she wanted to find a recipe for it and try it out.

The moment she tilted the thermal pot to fill Zelda's cup she heard a ripping noise and felt the garnet-colored sleeve of her left arm give way, inviting a draft to seep through a large gap in the back of her georgette blouse. Oops! She stood up straight, feeling the heat of embarrassment on her face and hoping no one noticed her wardrobe malfunction.

Marie must have heard it, though, judging by the sly, Mona Lisa smile that snuck across her face. At the same time, she reached under the table and gave Zelda a nudge. Zelda spoke something in French, presumably translating the bill of fare for dinner, but Marie's expression suggested that Zelda hadn't sounded convincing enough. Wrinkling her nose in distaste, Marie put her latte down and left the table in a huff.

Well, I guess you can't please all of the people even some of the time around here, Kim thought disgustedly as she excused herself and retreated to the bedroom to find another garment. This time she selected a silver silk and cashmere sweater, hoping it would hold together, and went to the kitchen to prepare a light breakfast for the group. Marie, however, didn't rejoin them.

*   *   *

Two hours later, after making breakfast and thoroughly cleaning the kitchen, Kim and Rock met in the hallway to go down to her place to dismantle the tree and pack up all of her decorations.

He came out of the bedroom wearing a red and black flannel shirt and a pair of worn jeans that hugged his body as though he'd painted them on. "Hey," he said in a deep, sexy voice on their way to the elevator, "I didn't get a chance to say this before, but you looked great in that red blouse. Why did you change?"

Kim glanced at the partially open door to Marie's room, wondering if the nurse stood behind it, listening. "I needed something warmer to wear. I felt a *chill* in the dining room."

He pressed the elevator button and flashed a disarming smile. "Why didn't you say so? I would have ignited the fireplace. Better yet, I would have kept you warm."

A loud thud echoed from the nurse's room, sounding like something had just hit the wall.

The elevator door silently parted and they stepped in. Kim didn't speak until the doors closed again.

"I'm going to strangle that nurse if she doesn't quit brooding about everything. She's supposed to be an asset to your mother, not a drag on her morale."

They stood side by side, watching the numbers on the overhead panel slowly decrease.

Rock chuckled. "You don't know Zelda. It's probably the other way around."

"Did you know Marie is wearing a wig? Something strange is going on with that girl. She's hiding more than just her true hair color. I can feel it in the negative vibes coming off her every time I'm around her." Kim studied Rock's face to catch his reaction. "Do you think she's in the country illegally? Gosh, I wonder if Zelda knows that."

He glanced down at her, arching one brow and silently confirming that he didn't need to answer that...

When the elevator reached the parking garage, Rock stepped out and held the doors open with his hand. "I'll get the flatbed from the utility room and meet you at your place."

Kim nodded and headed toward the public elevator bank to go up to the sixth floor. Once in her living room, she propped the door open for Rock to roll the flatbed through without beating up the woodwork then she stretched out on the loveseat.

Oh, if only I could curl up on this sofa for the rest of the day!

She closed her eyes for a moment and the next thing she knew, Rock stood over her, his lips close to her ear. Somewhere in the background, Nat King Cole's deep, velvety voice softly filled the air with a Christmas song about chestnuts and an open fire.

"Wake up, sleeping beauty, or I just might join you."

She reluctantly opened her eyes and found herself staring into his smiling face. How different he seemed since the last time they'd met here. He'd lost the cocky attitude for one thing. "How long have I been asleep?"

He took her hands and gently pulled her to a sitting position. "I'd say about ten minutes. It didn't take you long to go into hibernation. Here," he said and offered her a flute of sparkling liquid that had been sitting on the coffee table, "have a glass of bubbly."

"Ugh." She pushed it away. "It's too early for champagne."

He laughed and held the glass to her lips. "It's only ginger ale from your refrigerator. Here, have a sip. It might help clear your head."

Thinking he might be right, she accepted the glass and sampled it. The chilled, fresh liquid tasted so good she drank half the glass. "Did you meet anyone in the hallway as you were pulling the flatbed?"

He shook his head. "Not a soul. The place seems deserted. Everybody must be sleeping off the booze they consumed at the association party last night."

She sipped her soda. "At least something is going our way for a change."

Rock settled in next to her and placed his arm along the back of the loveseat. They sat quietly watching the multi-colored lights on the tree twinkle to the music. "That's a beautiful tree," he said thoughtfully. "It's a shame we have to take it apart."

"Don't you think it'll look just as nice in front of the patio doors in your penthouse? Not only that, but it'll hide the damage to your drapes."

He curled his arm around her shoulders and pulled her close. "Probably, but it won't be just you and me up there." He captured her gaze. "I enjoy sitting here alone with you."

Something in the way he whispered those words began to melt her heart and she wished they could spend the day together on this loveseat, shutting out the rest of the world. She sighed, wanting to curl up under his arm and press her cheek into his warm, inviting shoulder. He'd never made any secret of the fact that he wanted to be more than a friend. She couldn't deny that she wanted to deepen their relationship, too, but she held back, knowing she couldn't give herself to a one-night stand with this man, or five nights, if his mother chose to stick around that long. Once Zelda packed up and left for Vail,

76

Kim's agreement with Rock would conclude and it would be time for her to leave, too. No matter what happened between them, it would be over.

At least this way I'll depart on my own terms with my dignity intact, she thought grimly.

She didn't naively believe in fairytale endings the way her mother had. A man didn't fall in love with a woman just because they slept together. If that were true, Veronica would have had too many marriage offers to count.

Pushing those *happy* thoughts aside, she set the empty flute on the coffee table and stood. "If I don't start moving, I just might fall asleep sitting up. I'll get the boxes."

Rock stood up and examined the seven-foot balsam fir, loaded with decorations. "Gee, I don't know where to start."

Kim went to the closet to drag a stack of plastic storage cartons out and as she bent over, the seat of her pants gave way, parting with a loud tearing sound. She shot up straight, placing her hands over the gaping hole in her backside. "What the heck is going on with this outfit?"

Rock shrugged, but the sparkle in his eyes hinted that he could barely contain himself from the sight of her hot pink panties peeking through the hole.

"Well," Kim said with as much dignity as a person could with her booty on display, "I'm going to change." She briskly sidestepped past him, making sure he only saw her front as she hurried by. "I thought you said Diona's clothes were fine quality. I hope she got them on clearance."

A couple minutes later, she emerged from the bedroom wearing a similar pair of black slacks. "All fixed." She busied herself taking ornaments off the tree, glad to put the incident behind her.

They worked quietly side-by-side for a few minutes, sorting and packing decorations, some dating back to her childhood.

"This is interesting," Rock said and held up a small, hand-painted rocking horse made of delicate glass. "Where did you get it?"

Kim took the fragile ornament and gently cradled it in her palm as bittersweet memories filled her heart. "Glen Foster gave it to me for Christmas the year he and my mother dated," she said softly. "I must have been seven or eight at the time; just a pipsqueak, as he used to call me. I really grew attached to him. He brought me presents all the time and treated me like his own daughter. I took it harder than Veronica did when he left us."

She wrapped the item in a piece of tissue paper and laid it carefully in the storage box. "He never even said goodbye; not to me, anyway."

She reached for a crystal icicle hanging on a branch just above her head and couldn't quite grasp it. Rock stepped behind her. Laying one hand on her shoulder, he stretched his other hand above her head, hooking the icicle with his finger. He lifted it off the branch and handed it to her. His hand left her shoulder and slid snugly around her waist. Gently gripping her chin with his thumb and forefinger, he tilted her face toward him. "Maybe the man thought it best to simply leave. You were so young you probably wouldn't have understood his reasons."

She paused, considering his suggestion. "You know, I never thought of it that way."

He gave her a little squeeze as he gazed into her eyes. "Sometimes things aren't what they seem. Or people."

"Meaning you?"

He rested his forehead against hers. "I'm not as bad as you think I am."

"I never said you were bad," she said with a twinge of regret, "just wrong for me."

Brenda Lee's song about rocking around the Christmas tree came on the stereo. Suddenly Rock grabbed her hand. "C'mon, I'll show you what a great guy I can be," he said and led her in a lively swing dance around her living room.

She laughed as he skillfully maneuvered her through the steps. "I didn't know you could dance like this!"

"I learned it on a cruise," he said and guided her into an outside underarm turn, bringing his left arm over her head while pivoting her away from him. "There are a lot of things you don't know about me, all of which are good."

They danced around the room, rocking their way between the living room furniture, the tree and the dining room table. Once the song ended, they fell onto a loveseat, gasping for breath and thirsty, but not too tired to laugh at their own spontaneity.

Breathing hard, Rock unbuttoned the front of his shirt to let in some cool air then opened another can of soda and refilled their glasses. "Whew. I haven't danced like that in a long time." He held up his glass, motioning a toast. "I declare that we're going to have a good old-fashioned family Christmas. I'm determined to enjoy the rest of this week, no matter what happens. How about you?"

Kim touched the rim of her glass against his and laughed, just grateful that she'd changed her slacks before he whirled around the room. "Whatever you say, Sparky."

Rock set her glass on the coffee table. "I have that movie, you know. Diona left a stack of DVDs in the family room and *Christmas Vacation* happened to be one of them."

"I've heard people talk about it and say some of the lines, like the one I just quoted, but I've never watched it, myself."

He gave her an incredulous look. "You mean to tell me you've never seen *National Lampoon's Christmas Vacation*?"

She laughed. "No, but by the look on your face, I guess I should have."

"Well, I can fix that. After dinner, I'm sitting you down in the family room and we're watching it together. We'll get Mother and her nurse to join us. We can't go anywhere until the weather improves so we might as well enjoy what we have at home."

She smiled at his enthusiasm. "Then we'd better get going because we've got a lot to do before I start cooking again."

He pulled her to her feet. "Speaking of food, I want to thank you for that terrific meal you made last night. You're a fabulous cook. Mother really enjoyed it." He slid his arms around her waist facing her. "I did, too."

The scent of his cologne filled her nostrils, jarring her thoughts as she struggled to stay on task. She knew he wanted her to glide her arms around his neck, but instead she placed her palms on his chest, keeping him at bay. "I love to cook, and since we're on the subject, I can't wait to use your Artisan stand mixer to whip the potatoes."

His brows furrowed in confusion. "My...what?"

"Your mixer is that apple green appliance sitting on the counter in your kitchen. You know—that heavy-duty thing with the stainless steel mixing bowl? I've always wanted one exactly like that. If you don't mind, I'd love to borrow it sometime."

"You can use it any time you want," he murmured in a husky tone, "as long as you borrow me as well, to have dinner with you."

His slow, sexy drawl sounded so tempting, she began to falter. Dinner with him, alone, sounded heavenly, but... Weak-kneed and breathless, she pulled back and swallowed hard, shaken by the growing desire in his deep brown eyes. "Rock, I—"

His BlackBerry began to chirp in his jean pocket. He let it ring several times, but it kept making noise. With an irritated sigh, he let go of her and shook his head as he pulled out his phone. "Hello, *Mother*. Yes, we're on our way. See you soon." He shoved it back into his pocket, looking frustrated over the interruption. "She's bored and wants to know what's taking us so long."

"I guess I'd be bored, too, if the only person I had to talk to didn't talk at all," Kim said dryly and began to grab ornaments off the tree.

Though she made sure not to show it, she secretly thanked Zelda for the intrusion. The less time she spent with Zelda's son away from Mama Bear's watchful eyes, the better. It would be so easy to give in to Rock's charm here, in the privacy of her own home and allow him to sweep her into the moment, but it wouldn't be as easy to forget him when it was all over. And forget him she must because after this week, they'd simply be neighbors again. He'd go back to his corporate, jet-set lifestyle and she'd be merely someone he'd slept with for a week.

She began packing up faster than ever.

Chapter 7

That afternoon...

"Straighten that branch, my dear. It's making the tree look lopsided."

Zelda sat on the sofa, drinking tea and snacking on a plate of cookies, or biscuits, as she called them. She pointed at the crooked limb in question on the artificial tree standing in front of the wall of windows as Rock adjusted the top section. "Fix that garland near the bottom, too. It's twisted."

Kim grew up having a real tree at Christmastime, but the association had ruled against the residents using organic pine trees, declaring them a fire hazard. So, she'd ordered a top-of-the-line tree, complete with twinkle lights, on the Internet instead. It looked as close to the real thing as she had ever seen and very beautiful when fully trimmed. She just hadn't bargained on decorating it twice in two weeks.

"Here, take these," Zelda barked as she handed Kim a box of multi-colored ornaments. Ever since Kim and Rock walked into the living room navigating the cart, Zelda had been digging through the boxes, plucking out items and ordering people around from her spot on the sofa—thoroughly enjoying herself as the project manager of the Christmas tree development plan. Rock didn't seem to notice his mother's brusqueness, but Kim had to bite her lip to keep from saying something she might regret later. Or maybe not...

The sooner they put this tree back together, the sooner she could disappear into the kitchen, her private domain away from Zelda's bossiness and Marie's annoying flirting. Besides meatloaf and mashed potatoes, she planned to make cheesy cauliflower and bake something for dessert. With any luck, her work would keep her busy until dinnertime. One could only hope!

Rock had uncorked a bottle of Chianti that he'd borrowed from her wine rack back at the condo and poured her a glass. She'd refused at first, but at his insistence, she accepted a couple ounces, wondering if he'd pressed a glass in her hand to get her to loosen up around his mother and that goose of a nurse. Ironically, the first sip tasted wonderfully good. So did the next one and before she knew it, Rock had replenished her empty glass.

Zelda pulled a flat box out of a red and white storage container at her feet and shoved it at the nurse. She said something to Marie in French then added in English, presumably as an afterthought, "And be careful, they're crystal."

They're Swarovski crystal, Kim thought and sipped her wine. The set of twelve handcrafted icicles came from a little shop in St. Mark's Square in Venice, Italy, a present to Veronica from one of her lovers.

Marie took the box, adjusted her oversized glasses and began to circle the tree, hanging the fragile pieces as she hummed along with the Christmas music playing on the stereo. She looked like the dead had come to life in her milk-white dress, pale skin and mousey wig, not to mention the fact that she was actually *moving around* instead of parking her skinny butt on the sofa, expecting someone to serve her. Someone called Kim.

Marie ducked under Rock's arm then straightened, positioning her face mere inches from his. She smiled coyly and slowly turned away, as if coaxing him to follow her. He didn't seem to notice and instead kept unrolling a spool of glittery gold ribbon around the tree.

Kim pretended to be engrossed in spacing out the different colors of ornaments, all the while surreptitiously keeping an eye on the white tornado. The nurse's tacky ploy to get Rock's attention began to wear thin on her right away. Maybe she was just feeling the effects of good wine, but she had the unmistakable urge to take those icicles away from Marie and shove them where the sun didn't shine. In the end, her manners prevailed and instead of behaving like an immature teenager, she busied herself to keep her mind off things she shouldn't be thinking. Rock didn't belong to her and if he wanted to flirt with that idiot of a nurse, she didn't have a right to become jealous or interfere. Yeah, but just the same, she wanted to!

She took a step backward to get a good look at her progress and nearly fell over Roscoe. The tubby tabby had positioned himself right behind her, engrossed in watching the activity, but when she stepped on his paw, he scooted between her legs with a yowl, almost tripping her. She staggered a couple steps before Rock caught her in his arms.

"Are you okay?" His piercing dark eyes studied her face with concern.

She smiled, placing her palms on his broad chest as a warm, languorous glow spread through her being. "I am *now*..."

"Roscoe, come here!"

Zelda sat forward and imperiously waved her arm. The cat ignored her and trotted across the living room then leaped onto the coffee table where he sat with ears perked, eyes wide, mesmerized by the lights twinkling on the tree.

Kim quickly glanced around, looking for Sasha and found the dog on Rock's desk, sitting in her tote with her head peeking out, being quiet like a good little girl.

Breathing a sigh of relief, she went back to hanging ornaments. Things were getting a little fuzzy, but what the heck. Happy holidays! That wine seemed to hit the spot.

Marie spun around with the empty box in her hands and Kim ducked just in time, narrowly avoiding the nurse's elbow from jamming her in the face and possibly giving her a black eye. Casting a wicked look in Marie's direction, Kim grabbed her wine glass off the coffee table and moved to Rock's side, wedging him between them. She needed a referee before she turned the witch-in-white into a Chianti-flavored candy cane.

She tossed back the rest of her wine and pointed the empty glass at the tree. "Rock, what do you think of my progress so far?"

He stopped adjusting another branch and smiled. "It looks perfect, honey, but then I know I can always count on you to do the right thing."

She looked into his gorgeous brown eyes, unable to curb the persistent smile tugging at the corners of her mouth as another surge of elation spread through her. Did he say *honey*? Hey, he'd never called her *that* before...

"Diona," Zelda snapped and held up the Royal Albert teapot she'd purchased at the Mall of America yesterday. "Brew some more hot water for my tea."

Everyone turned toward Zelda, and for a moment, an awkward silence prevailed.

Oh, she means me!

Kim shoved her glass at Rock then almost jumped over an ornament box standing between her and the empty teapot. She'd been so preoccupied with her complaints against Marie that for a moment she forgot the main issue—pretending to be Rock's wife.

"More hot tea coming right up," she said, staring straight ahead, as she marched into the kitchen. She couldn't look anyone in the eye, especially Zelda, for fear she'd give herself away.

A couple minutes later, she returned with a steaming teapot and an attitude adjustment, resolved to put up a confident front in spite of her faux pas. Her good intentions didn't last long.

That gangly nurse stood too close to Rock to pass for merely being friendly as she reached up to place a lighted star atop the tree. She could obviously make the distance but chose to put on an act, trying to look helpless when her arm, supposedly, wouldn't stretch that far. After rising on her tiptoes a couple times, Marie groaned in frustration, prompting Rock to put his current task on hold and give her some assistance. Her green eyes grew wide when his fingers brushed hers as the star changed hands. She leaned in his direction, her face moving close enough to his to kiss him, her gaze focused on his mouth.

"Excuse me!"

Kim charged past Roscoe, ignoring his yowl and the big orange paw that suddenly took a swipe at her when she blocked his view of the tree. She set down the teapot with a thump then literally stomped over to the tree, elbowing her way between her man and her nemesis.

"I need to straighten these ornaments," she said to no one in particular, but just the same, her tone of voice carried a firm warning for a certain pain-in-the-patootie to stay out of her way. She reached for a shiny red bulb, but almost had it knocked out of her hand when Marie turned sharply, jamming her hip against Kim's. Lightheaded from the wine, Kim didn't realize she'd lost her balance until the objects around her began to tilt.

"Whoa." Rock steadied her with his hands on her shoulders and repositioned her to face him. "Guess what I found."

Still a bit dizzy, she looked up and saw a sprig of mistletoe dangling above her head.

"Look at me."

She stared into his dark eyes and forgot everything else, captivated by the tenderness and devotion he held for only her. Instinctively she slid her palms up his chest, circling his neck. He responded by sliding his wide hands around her waist, gently pulling her close.

"Merry Christmas, my darling."

Their faces were but a breath apart. His gaze dropped seductively to her mouth as he angled his head and placed a deep, passionate kiss upon her lips.

She was stunned at first, taken completely by surprise. She'd expected a peck on the cheek, but the moment their mouths melded together, her pulse shift into high gear, crystallizing her senses and sending a message loud and clear to her brain that this was no ordinary smooch. No kiss had ever made her heart flutter so fast, had ever made her body respond *like this*.

Zelda cleared her throat.

Kim ignored it as the stress of the last few days ebbed away and the sheer pleasure of being in Rock's strong arms gave her a secure feeling she never wanted to end.

In other words, the old bat could wait.

Zelda cleared her throat again with pronounced impatience.

Something behind them crashed. The clang startled Sasha, sending her into a barking frenzy as Roscoe dived off the table and scuttled under the tree. Kim gave startled cry and yanked herself away from Rock's arms. He refused to release his arm around her at first and looked shaken as though it had upset him to let her go.

Marie had dropped a cluster of silver bells on the floor, but it had obviously caught on the edge of the coffee table on the way down. She stood with her arms folded, her oversized glasses perched on the end of her nose, looking put out.

That did it.

Kim literally got in her face. "What's your problem, anyway?"

"Now, now, darling," Rock said softly and pulled her away from Marie. Spinning her around, he nudged her in the direction of their bedroom. "Don't get upset over something so small. I'm sure she didn't mean it."

Kim looked back at the mess in the living room. "But, what about the—"

Rock pulled her into the bedroom and shut the door. "Marie can finish up."

He walked her to the bed and drew back the covers.

"Wait, wait," she practically shouted and backed away, waving her arms. "You're crazy if you think I'm going to jump into this bed with you while your mother is sitting out there—"

"We aren't jumping into anything right now. *You* are going to take a nap. I would never take advantage of a woman in your present state."

"Look, I'm not tired anymore and I haven't had much wine—"

He picked her up like a fragile doll and gently placed her in the bed. "Sweet dreams, my darling." He kissed her on the forehead and pulled the covers over her.

The last thing she heard was Rock shutting the door behind him.

Chapter 8

I've got a secret...

Kim reclined in bed, staring at the weather report on television while struggling to hold down her dinner. She didn't know what had brought it on, but the meatloaf and mashed potatoes she'd served for the evening meal now smoldered like a Yule log in her stomach. She shouldn't have eaten that second lemon curd tart while watching *Christmas Vacation*, either. Topped with real whipped cream, it had tasted heavenly with fresh brewed coffee, but now the rich dessert soured in the back of her throat.

Maybe it was the wine, she thought with regret as she swallowed hard, wincing at not only how much she'd unwittingly consumed that afternoon while decorating the tree, but ultimately at what a fool she'd made of herself in front of everyone when she'd pitched a fit at Marie.

Ugh, I'll never allow myself to engage in such pettiness ever again.

Rock came out of the bathroom wearing his Joe Boxer pajama bottoms and a milk-white T-shirt that clung to his damp body. Suddenly the snow totals and wind chills on television were no longer important as her gaze lingered on his taut, muscular chest, taking in the perfect symmetry of his physique, a tribute to his daily workout. Damp, wavy black hair fell thick across his forehead. A day's growth of beard shadowed his face. His dark eyes, shuttered with thick lashes, regarded her lazily.

No wonder Diona had fallen in love with him.

Their gazes lingered briefly when a sudden sparkle in his eyes reminded her that her actions were giving him the wrong idea. Embarrassed, she glanced away and focused on the bare wall. But something didn't look right. Wasn't a picture or a plaque supposed to be hanging in that empty spot above the loveseat?

A wave of nausea washed up the back of her throat, overriding her thoughts.

"You cooked another awesome dinner tonight," Rock said evenly and walked over to the bed, acting as though the day had gone without a hitch.

"Thank you," she managed to reply.

"I ate too much again, though." He picked up the remote and pressed the power button, turning it off.

"Someone had to pick up the slack for Marie. I don't know how she can live on two tablespoons of mashed potatoes. That's all I saw her eat tonight."

"She's finicky." He raised one brow as he placed the remote back on the nightstand. "Are you feeling all right?"

"I—I'm fine," she said, not knowing why she had a problem telling him the truth. "I'm just tired, that's all."

"Me, too." He punched up his pillows, taking care not to disturb the dog perched on the one separating them. Instead of growling at Rock, Sasha leaned over and licked his hand. He gently patted her on the head then pulled back the covers and slid into bed. "I took a sleeping pill to make sure I get some decent shut-eye tonight. My schedule is booked tight tomorrow so I've got to get plenty of rest." He smiled and extended his palm. "Good night, darling. Sleep well."

She blinked in surprise at his genuine sincerity before slipping her hand in his. "Yeah, good night," she whispered as they shook hands.

Rock turned off the light and turned his back to her then pulled the comforter over his head and exhaled a deep sigh.

Kim lay in the darkness, listening to the tempo of his breathing slowly relax as he slipped into a deep sleep. What happened to the sexy guy who tried everything he could think of to seduce her on their first night together? When did he change into a sensitive, caring man who not only respected her privacy, but her dog's personal space as well?

That's what you wanted, she thought, wondering why the realization had immediately produced a surge of disappointment.

A tiny, wet nose pressed against the side of her face, creating a sweet diversion from her thoughts. "Nighty-night, baby doll," she whispered and rubbed Sasha's chin with the tip of her finger. Sasha responded with a lick on her nose and inched close enough to lie against Kim's cheek.

Minutes turned into a half hour then an hour as Kim lay with her eyes closed, trying to go to sleep. Her stomach began to gurgle for the umpteenth time. She sat up in discomfort, clutching her arm around her waist as a groan escaped her lips.

I need some Seven Up, she thought, hoping the lemon-lime soda would settle it down. Rock probably had something more potent in his medicine cabinet, but she didn't want to disturb him by rummaging around in his bathroom, possibly dropping things on the marble floor and disrupting the peaceful atmosphere in the room.

She sat up and slowly pulled the covers off as her bare legs swung over the side of the bed. Her pink chenille robe lay across the end of the mattress. Groping in the dark, she snatched it and shoved her bare arms into the soft, thick fabric before goose bumps could travel up her skin. The thin, sleeveless nightgown she wore tonight offered little warmth outside of Rock's down comforter.

"Stay, Sasha," she whispered and placed her hand on the dog's tiny chest. "You be a good girl and keep Rock company. I'll be right back."

Without looking back to make sure the dog obeyed, she tiptoed across the carpet and slipped out the door. The hallway looked eerily deserted in the shadowed light, but at the same time, she didn't feel alone. No matter, she had to get something to calm her stomach.

The icy marble flooring chilled her toes as she tied the sash around her waist and padded toward the family room, wishing she'd taken the time to locate her bunny slippers and put them on. Nearing the patio doors, she caught a whiff of cigarette smoke and her ire grew at the Robertsons.

Don't they ever give it a rest?

A wave of cold air surrounded her like a frigid blanket, causing her to shiver uncontrollably. In the silvery light, the drapes covering the sliding glass door to the balcony wafted slightly.

Well, no wonder the floor feels like an ice rink, she thought. *Someone left the patio door open...*

She reached out to pull the curtain aside but stopped short, forgetting all about closing the door.

"Mercy, it's cold out here," Zelda's British accent cut through the night. "I'll never complain about the heat in St. Petersburg again."

"That's what I've been saying all along. Why should we sneak out here to have a drink and freeze our butts off while she has the run of the house?"

Wha-what?

Kim started at the introduction of a completely new voice. It sounded familiar, but she couldn't identify it. With slow caution, she gripped the fabric, peering past the edge of the drape, all the while struggling to refrain herself from the urge to gasp.

Marie and Zelda sat at the patio table, bundled up in coats and blankets. Zelda reposed regally like a queen on her throne wrapped in her full-length chinchilla. She held a goblet of white wine in one hand, a lit cigarette in the other. Marie wore a fur-trimmed bonnet, sans the oversized spectacles, making it difficult to recognize her, but her gray wool coat gave her away. She raised a stemmed glass of wine to her lips.

"You know I can't smoke in the house." Zelda took a quick drag on her cigarette. "Have patience, my dear. It won't be long now."

"It's been too long already!" Marie set her wine glass on the table with a thump and glared at Zelda. "She's getting on my nerves."

Zelda chuckled as she drank her wine, making a wry sound, as if to imply that Marie's complaint was an understatement.

Marie swatted a gloved hand through the air, chasing away a few errant snowflakes. "We should have confronted her today when she tried to start something. It would have been a pleasure to throw that imposter out."

Kim shivered at the realization that they knew she and Rock were pretending to be married. Really, well then why hadn't they announced it and ended this stupid affair?

Zelda took another drag on her cigarette then waved the notion away as she exhaled, creating a billow of white smoke. "There's plenty of time for that. I'm not due to fly out until Wednesday. Besides, we need to make sure we have a solid case or the whole thing will blow up in our faces."

"I'll probably strangle her if I have to put up with her for that long." Marie threw off her blanket and stood up. "This is ridiculous. We're freezing out here!" She kicked at a mound of snow next to the table. "I'm going inside to finish my drink in the den and I don't care who sees me." She picked up the wine bottle and shoved it under her arm. "I'm not putting up with this any longer, Zelda. If you don't confront that woman and expose her by tomorrow night, *I will*."

Zelda grunted. "Not so fast. I've got just as much at stake here as you do. We'll handle this my way."

"The longer it goes on, the worse it gets! Every time those two start acting all *kissy-face*, I want to scream!"

That's Diona, Kim thought and wondered why she hadn't realized it before. All of the facts surrounding her odd presence fit—the obsession with Rock, the jealousy, the refusal to speak.

But, that voice...where had Kim heard it before? The ultra-feminine, high-pitched tone, almost to the point of sounding whiny, nagged at her memory; but for some reason, she couldn't put a face or name to it.

"Don't you dare," Zelda replied firmly. "We must approach this intelligently and that means gathering all the facts. In the morning, before we go shopping, we'll stop by the front desk to have another friendly chat with that gossipy security guard. He's full of very useful information." She rose from the chair, completely unassisted, and took one last drag on her cigarette then tossed it over the balcony. "Come along. Let's go back to my room and chat while we finish our wine." She turned toward the patio door. "I have a feeling I'm going to need a few *bevies* before this is all over."

Hearing that, Kim spun away from the door and sprinted through the living room, not stopping until she stood safely inside Rock's bedroom. The room was quiet except for the slow, methodical hum of his breathing. A soft glow from his clock radio cast a blue light, providing just enough for her to make out the silhouette of his long, sinewy body burrowed peacefully under the comforter on his side of the bed.

Sasha jumped off her pillow and trotted to the edge of the mattress, whimpering softly.

Kim scooped her up and hurried into the bathroom, shutting the door quickly behind her before snapping on the light. She dropped the dog into the litter box and sat on the edge of the Jacuzzi tub then covered her mouth with both hands as she burst out with an astonished laugh.

94

"Can you believe that?" she said in a high-pitched whisper to Sasha as the dog squatted in her box and looked into her eyes. "What a couple of con artists! And they called *me* an imposter!"

Sasha simply stared, apparently unmoved by the latest developments as she tinkled on the scented litter.

"Zelda smokes, drinks and gets a free ride everywhere in that rented wheelchair because she's got Rock convinced that she's living on borrowed time. What's her motive for faking?" Kim shook her head, wishing she knew. "And as for that brainless nurse—the *real* Diona," Kim snapped as she gripped the edge of the tub, "she'd better think twice about exposing me. I don't know what those two are up to, Sasha, but the game is over. Tomorrow when Rock gets home from work, it's going to end, and it may not be pretty, but the time for laying all our cards on the table has come." She let out a deep breath. "You know what? I am *so* glad this ordeal is almost over. I hate deceiving people. It's about time the truth came out."

But...what was the truth? Why did Zelda go to such lengths to make her son think she could die at any moment? That's what Kim wanted to know. Not only that, but how did that witless prima Dona sidekick of hers fit into the situation? Did she really think she could get her fiancé back by making him look like a fool?

Sasha finished taking care of business and jumped out of the litter box. She trotted across the white and gray marble floor, the clickety-clack of her nails echoing about the room. Kim picked up the dog, nestling Sasha in the warmth of her lap.

"Zelda said she had a lot at stake," Kim murmured while she stroked Sasha's back. "What did she mean by that? Whatever it is, it must be very important to make her go to such an extreme. This charade of hers, though, seems uncharacteristic for someone who has always held the winning hand. She must be absolutely desperate for something." Kim slipped her hands around Sasha's tummy and lifted the chubby little canine to eye level. "Like me. I'll sell out and move before I'll give you up."

She kissed the dog's nose as her thoughts drifted toward the inevitable showdown.

"Ladies, plan your words carefully. Don't think you're going to turn the tables and make this deception of yours all about me," she declared to herself. "I haven't survived ten years of nursing by being a wimp. No one is going to assassinate my character to prove a point, whatever that may be. I'm ready for your ambush with both barrels loaded and cocked. *Merry Christmas*, ladies. This is one fight I intend to win!"

Chapter 9

Monday morning, December 21

Kim awoke the next morning to the heavy beat of a Guns and Roses song blasting from Rock's clock radio. She groggily opened one eye as a long arm, clothed in a blue, two-toned striped shirt, reached out and shut off the noise.

"Sorry about that," Rock said sweetly as he straightened and slipped into a dark suit coat. "I meant to turn it off as soon as I woke up." He gave her a warm smile and adjusted his shirt cuffs. "I always seem to wake up just before my alarm goes off, but I guess I got enough sleep last night because I've been up for almost an hour now."

The good-natured purr of his deep, sexy voice drew her out of her sleepy haze. She opened both eyes to see him standing over her, dressed like the executive he was, readying himself for a busy day at the office.

"Oh, that's okay," she murmured before being overtaken with a huge yawn. "I should get up, anyway, and feed the dog." She checked the pillow next to her head where the plump little Chihuahua usually slept and found it vacant. "Where's Sasha?"

"Gee, I don't know." He glanced around the room. "She's around here somewhere. I put a small chunk of that canned food you had on the dresser in her dish and she's been following me around ever since."

Is that so? Kim suppressed a small smile.

"Would you like some coffee? I've got a fresh pot brewing in the kitchen."

"Um, sure," she replied shyly and stretched her arms above her head, "that sounds wonderful." Thankfully, her stomach problems were gone this morning.

Once Rock left the room, Kim sat up and fluffed the pillows behind her then ran her fingers through her hair to smooth out the cowlick she knew was plastered to the back of her head. She sat back and drew a deep breath, wondering what had gotten into Rock. His sweet, solicitous behavior seemed so different from the Rock of four days ago. She didn't know what to think. Did he always treat the women in his life like this? Could this be a preview of what it would like to be his wife in the true sense?

If that's true—mister, I don't want to give you up.

"Don't be ridiculous," she said aloud to herself. "He's being nice because you're doing him a huge favor. There's nothing between you and him but neighborly friendship and a handshake."

But when Rock appeared a few minutes later, his actions didn't come close to the definition of neighborly.

"Here you are, darling." He spoke tenderly as he handed her a mug of steaming coffee and a saucer containing a lemon bar and a slice of cranberry bread. "I hope you like these. It's all that's left of that platter of desserts Mrs. Doyle gave you." He pulled a folded napkin from his suit pocket and spread it across her lap. "I'm afraid Mother enjoyed it so much she's eaten most of it already."

"Thank you," Kim replied as she took the small plate. "I actually saved you a few frosted brownies because I know you like them. They're in the freezer." It was the only place they were safe from Zelda's ravenous appetite.

Rock caressed her cheek with the back of his hand. "Baby, you're so good to me. I'm going to miss getting so much attention when this is all over."

Speaking of the situation being all over...

She seriously considered the idea of leveling with him about Zelda, but sounds of someone making a racket in the hallway quickly distracted her.

"That must be Mother. She probably wants some coffee. Excuse me," Rock said and promptly left the room.

Kim drank her coffee and ate her breakfast in silence, strangely sobered by the realization that tomorrow morning she would most likely wake up in her own bed...alone. For the first time ever, she realized what an isolated existence she lived. Sure, she had a lot of friends and many of her neighbors were as close as family, but that didn't change the fact that she kept house all by herself, with no one to wake up to, no one to have dinner with or to snuggle with on frigid nights. And for the first time, she understood the reason for the hollow feeling inside her.

Before she could blink them back, tears smarted in her eyes.

*   *   *

A few minutes later, Kim washed her face then dressed in her favorite black leggings and a green tunic.

No more borrowed designer clothes for me, she thought rebelliously as she pulled on her suede ankle booties. She'd take her comfortable clothes any day over fancy clothes that fell apart. Besides, those things didn't match her personality. She'd never be the kind of glamour girl that Rock found irresistible, and now that the truth was almost out, she was through pretending, through trying to be someone she wasn't.

She slipped on her earrings, tiny red Christmas bells, fluffed her blonde hair then walked into the dining room, ignoring the stares of all three people sitting around the oval table.

"Good morning," she said to no one in particular and stepped into the kitchen to pour a fresh cup of French roast. She reappeared in a moment with her Santa mug and surveyed the crowd. Rock sat at the head of the table with a tall mug of coffee and the Wall Street Journal spread in front of him. Marie/Diona peered sourly over the rim of her juice glass through her ugly, oversized spectacles, glaring at Kim with her usual evil stare. Zelda sat in her wheelchair across from Marie/Diona, pretending to be oblivious to her so-called nurse's animosity as she munched on a piece of toast and marmalade.

Now that Kim knew the truth about these two, and their little game was about to be exposed, she couldn't wait to see Rock's reaction. She smiled at Zelda, fighting the temptation to spill the beans here and now. "Got plans for today?"

"As soon as I finish my breakfast, Marie and I are leaving straightaway for the Mall of America for a bit of shopping," Zelda replied, her voice sounding deeper than ever.

It must be from sneaking all those cigarettes on the balcony while strategizing "intelligent" ways to get rid of me, Kim thought cynically.

Zelda gave her a strange look, as though she could read Kim's thoughts. "And you?"

"Oh, I have personal errands to run and a few other things to catch up on," she said. Like sleep, for instance. Taking a nap in her own bed sounded like a wonderful idea.

Rock folded the paper and pushed back his chair. "I'd better get going." He motioned to Kim. "Will you walk with me to the elevator, darling?"

He leaned over and kissed his mother. "I'll have my assistant make reservations for dinner tonight at Origami. I'm hungry for some good sushi. Have a nice day shopping."

Zelda spun her chair around. "Marie, fetch my coat and pocketbook. We'll wait for the cab downstairs."

Rock slipped his arm around Kim's waist as they walked along. Dipping his head, he whispered in her ear. "Is something wrong? You seem preoccupied."

The tenderness in his voice nearly melted her resolve. She'd hardly slept all night, thinking about the situation. "I'm fine, really, but we need to talk."

He stopped mid-stride. "What's the matter?"

She couldn't tell him now, not with Zelda and Marie within earshot. "Rock, I—"

Thankfully, the buzzing of his BlackBerry cut her off. He pulled the device out of his pocket and checked the screen. "It's my senior data architect. Honey, I'm sorry, but I've got to take this call." He pressed the answer button and pressed the BlackBerry to his ear. "Yeah, Sean, what's up?" He paused for a couple moments, listening intently. "Yeah...yeah..." He opened the closet and grabbed his coat. "Is that going to cause a problem?" He turned toward the elevator and pressed the call button.

"See you tonight. I'll call you this afternoon," he whispered to her and kissed her on the lips as the doors silently swished open. He lingered the slightest moment, though, before pulling away. Slinging the coat over his shoulder, he entered the elevator, engrossed once again in his phone conversation.

"Well, how do you feel about that," he said in a business tone as the doors closed on him.

I'll be waiting, she thought somberly, because she missed him already.

*   *   *

Stepping into the foyer that evening, Rock loosened his tie and breathed a tired sigh. What a killer of a day he'd endured. One of his best managers had resigned to take a position with a competitor, he'd received notice that a major account had filed bankruptcy and for the first time ever, he'd had words with his assistant when she accidentally hung up on a client during an important conference call. It wasn't her fault. Everyone had experienced problems trying to adjust to the new phone system. He knew he'd have to make peace with her tomorrow and make things right, but tonight all he wanted to do was relax and have dinner with the people he cared about the most.

He never got the chance to call Kim, either, as he'd promised. She'd wanted to talk to him about something before he left for the office this morning and it seemed important to her.

I need to find her.

He crossed the foyer and charged down the hallway, tossing his coat on a bench along the way. He needed to apologize for not making good on his word.

Besides that, he'd truly missed her—all day. He'd missed her sweet voice, her company, but most of all, he missed kissing her. Sometime in the last four days they'd changed from being merely neighbors fulfilling a bargain to close friends. He'd always wanted it to be more than that, but he'd botched things so badly in the beginning he knew it would take more than wearing clothes to bed and a hand-delivered cup of coffee in the morning to change her low opinion of him.

Zelda and Marie were in the living room, sitting in front of a cozy fire when he walked in. Multi-colored lights on the Christmas tree twinkled like sparkling gems.

"Sorry I'm late, Mother. I couldn't get away as soon as I'd planned, but we've still got enough time to get to the restaurant." Ignoring Marie, he walked past her and glanced around. "Where's Ki— I mean, my wife?"

Zelda set her mug on the coffee table and sat back, making room for Roscoe to leap into her lap. "Haven't seen her," she replied crisply and began stroking the spine of her furry orange monster. "Perhaps she's gone out."

"She wouldn't do that," Rock said, checking his watch. "We're due to leave for dinner in fifteen minutes." Or would she? Was that what she was trying to tell him this morning—that she'd changed her mind and wanted to move back to her own place?

Without a word, he left the living room and burst into his bedroom, hoping to find her napping or in the shower. He didn't find her in either place and frantically searched the room for clues to her disappearance. The bed looked freshly made, but most of Diona's things were missing from his closet—dresses, sweaters, even the shoes he used to trip over were mysteriously absent. What did she do, take the goods and run?

"No way," he said aloud. "I've still got her Christmas tree. She'd never abandon that—or my Artisan mixer." Just the same, he attempted to assure himself Kim hadn't left him by looking around for her dog. "Hey, mutt," he said and whistled softly. "Come here, little Sausage." He checked around the room and even looked under the bed. No dog, no dog carrier, either.

Suddenly, he heard the elevator doors swish open and he dashed into the hallway. Kim walked toward him carrying the dog's tote bag. She wore a simple black chemise with matching clutch purse, trimmed with sequins. The gown's slight contours accentuated her petite frame; the rounded neckline exposed her ivory skin and perfect bone structure. A diamond-studded pendant adorning her neck and matching drop earrings reflected the light like tiny electric sparks under the glow of the chandelier.

She set the pink tote on the floor to let the dog jump out.

"Well, look at you," Rock said, unable to hide his relief as he gazed into her clear blue eyes. He took her hand in his and twirled her around, making her laugh. "You look absolutely stunning." His words lit up her face. Her shimmering pink smile was radiant, and only for him. Without knowing why, he began to sing a couple bars of Frank Sinatra's song, "The Way You Look Tonight."

"You never called me today," she said with a thread of disappointment in her voice. "Didn't you miss me?"

He slid his arm around her waist and pulled her close, holding her left hand to his chest as he began to guide her in a waltz to imaginary music. "More than you know," he murmured in her ear then inhaled deeply, savoring the floral bouquet of her fragrance as he slowly guided her around the small, circular room. He couldn't remember the name of it—something to do with a walk in the moonlight—but knew the scent well from many visits to Victoria's Secret to purchase gifts.

"Rock, why are we dancing," she asked with a laugh. "It's fun, but there's no music. Not even that piped-in elevator stuff that's usually coming from the sound system in the ceiling."

"I like waltzing you around the room," he said honestly and pulled her closer, placing his chin on the top of her head. "It gives me an excuse to hold you in my arms."

They stood still for a moment, quietly embracing each other.

Then without warning, Kim turned to ice and pulled away, focused on something behind him.

"What's the matter? What happened?" Confused and caught off guard, he turned to see what had destroyed their intimate moment. Marie stood posed like a marble statue at the other end of the hallway—only the Venus de Milo she was not.

With fire in her eyes, Kim silently snatched The Sausage's carrier and walked away, cutting a detour through the kitchen to avoid Marie completely. Rock followed Kim, wondering what to do now. He'd waited all day to take his wife to dinner at a great seafood restaurant in downtown Minneapolis, but the chill in this place felt like Frostbite Falls, Minnesota and it had him wondering what would happen next. Problem employees he could handle. He'd had professional training for that. But, when it came to the women in his life, he didn't have a clue.

"My goodness, where have you been," Zelda said to Kim, displaying her usual bossiness as they entered the living room. "We must be on our way or we're going to be late." She blotted her lips with her monogrammed handkerchief and turned to him. "I need a bite to eat." She put a hand over her heart. "I'm feeling faint."

Rock looked up and did a double take at Kim's narrow-eyed stare.

"I went down to the security guard's office this afternoon. Monday is Al's day for his weekly blood pressure reading," Kim said to Zelda then cut a sideways glance at Marie. "Afterward we had a *nice* chat."

Zelda and Marie exchanged a knowing look. Kim folded her arms, but said no more, as though waiting for them to make the next move.

Oh-oh, Rock thought worriedly and pulled back his suit jacket, shoving his hands into his pockets. The cauldron of animosity bubbling between Kim and Marie indicated that something serious must have happened to blow Kim's cover.

The jig was up, as his mother would say.

*   *   *

Standing between Rock and Marie, Kim faced off with Zelda, waiting for the old lady to take the bait.

Zelda set Roscoe aside and sat up straight, looking pointedly at Kim. "Speaking of chats, Arnie Daye rang me up this morning." She folded her hands on her lap. "He said he's never heard of you or your mum."

Bingo...

From the corner of her eye, Kim saw Rock flinch. He'd have some serious explaining to do eventually, but that was his problem. He shouldn't have started down this road in the first place. Then again, Zelda wasn't going to escape unscathed, either. Not if she had anything to do with it.

"He's never heard of you because you aren't his niece," Zelda continued in a smug, authoritative tone. "You don't hail from the Vineyard and you're certainly not part of his social circle." She emphasized the words *social circle* as though growing up in any class other than the wealthiest five percent constituted a disgrace all by itself. "Perhaps it's time you confess who you really are and why you're sleeping with my son, pretending to be someone you're not."

Rock attempted physically to get between the women, but Kim quickly sidestepped him, letting him know that she intended to defend herself.

"I am Mrs. Rock Henderson," she said boldly, staring directly at Marie/Diona as she held up her left hand, showing off her four-carat chunk of ice.

"You wish!" Marie/Diona cried with a smug look and shoved Kim's hand away. "Zelda's attorney hired a private investigator to run a check on you. I emailed him a picture of you on Friday night with my cell phone. All he had to do was show it to Al Grabowski and the rest was easy." Marie/Diona gave her the once-over with a critical eye. "We know who you are."

"Well, well," Kim spouted dryly, "the mummy can speak."

Marie/Diona's eyes flared. "Shut up!"

"You did what?" Rock angrily shook his head, staring down at his mother. "So this is what you two have been up to..."

"Miss Stratton," Zelda said with authority, ignoring her son, "I suggest you drop the pretense, pack your bag and leave at once. Go back to your 'storage locker,' that modest condominium you occupy on the sixth floor and leave us alone. My son no longer needs your services."

"She's not going anywhere, Mother," Rock said and clasped his hand around Kim's, lacing his fingers between hers. "This is my home and I want her here—" he gazed intently into her eyes, "with me."

"If anyone should drop the pretense, it's you, Zelda," Kim said and pulled away from Rock while removing a flat box of cigarettes from her clutch. "Recognize these? I believe you left them in the pocket of your Chinchilla."

Zelda looked startled for a moment, but quickly composed herself. "Those are *old*. They've been tucked under my gloves for months."

"Oh, really?" Kim flashed her best killer smile, resisting the urge to burst out laughing. Gotcha! "Then you must like to smoke old cigarettes when you sit outside on the balcony in the middle of the night. They probably go better with your *old* wine."

Zelda's face flushed crimson with fury. "Don't try to change the subject, young lady, by turning the focus upon me. My conduct is not in question here. Your association with my son is."

Kim moved toward Zelda with her hands on her hips. "Excuse me, but your conduct is very much in question here! You had no right to violate my privacy by dispatching an investigator to weasel information out of the security guard in this building—the nicest guy in the world, I might add—for the sole purpose of prying into my background to assassinate my character. Even so, I have nothing to hide. I didn't grow up in Martha's Vineyard, but I do have relatives there and we did visit some of them once a year."

"An unfortunate situation, from what I understand," Zelda said, lowering her brows in genuine seriousness. "But then, if I had a daughter who'd foolishly squandered her entire inheritance on an unscrupulous man that I disapproved of and then had a child out of wedlock with him, I might be tempted to disown her as well. I must say, the man has made somewhat of a name for himself now, but I am told that you possess the common sense to have nothing to do with him and I at least give you credit for that."

What...?

Time stood still as Kim blinked in confusion. Spots appeared in front of her eyes and a strange buzzing invaded her head. Her knees began to tremble. She grabbed Rock's arm for support. What did Zelda just say?

Rock slid his arm across her back to assist her. "Darling, are you all right?"

She ignored him, focusing her attention on this earth-shattering revelation. She knew very little about Veronica's family and absolutely nothing about her biological father. Several times during her childhood and teenage years, Kim had asked her mother pointed questions about the people mysteriously absent in their lives, but Veronica refused to talk about them. She preferred to dwell on her current boyfriend instead.

Kim held on to her sanity for dear life and looked into Zelda's eyes. "You—you mean—you know the identity of my father?"

Zelda's flustered expression revealed her ignorance of the fact that Veronica had kept the man's name to herself until she died. No photos, no scrapbooks, not even a card or gift remained of her relationship with Kim's father.

The shock in Rock's eyes made it plain that his mother's announcement had taken him by surprise, too.

Suddenly, Kim realized her face must have broadcast the entire tragic story of her life because Zelda's neck and ears turned crimson.

"Don't you?"

"No," Kim said in a small voice, feeling like a lonely eight-year-old again. "I don't."

Marie/Diona burst out a triumphant laugh and glared disdainfully. "Well, that's one more reason why Rock could never marry you for real. Cinderella's story only works in the fairy tale. In this day and age, you must have more going for you than a cute face," she said as she haughtily looked Kim up and down, "and the wardrobe of a Keebler elf. You need to have *class*."

Kim let go of Rock and clenched her fists, tempted to rearrange Marie/Diona's perfect patrician nose, but put her hands behind her back instead as she got in the woman's face. "I'd rather look like a

Keebler elf than Norman Bates' mother!"

"I'm the genuine Diona, the one Rock loves!" Diona cried, ripping off her square, oversized glasses and ratty wig. She reached back and pulled a flat clip out of her hair, sending her thick, coppery tresses tumbling past her shoulders. Even with no makeup and pale skin, now that her true looks were exposed, she proved to be a ravishing beauty. The reddish hair, the whiny voice—it all came back to Kim now—in her mind's eye she saw Ann Margaret in an old Elvis film, *Viva Las Vegas.*

A true diva.

Suddenly, many things began to make sense, like the small disasters that had been plaguing Kim ever since she moved in with Rock.

"Those clothes you abandoned in Rock's closet," Kim said. "The seams didn't rip out by themselves, did they?" At Diona's smug laugh, Kim continued, "You sabotaged them, didn't you? You must have cut them with one of Rock's razor blades just to embarrass me and make me look stupid!"

Diona had also been the culprit who'd taken the picture of Rock at NASCAR, Kim thought as the blank wall space above the loveseat crossed her mind.

Diona smirked. "Remember the oil on the dining room floor? You looked so funny lying on your backside!"

All Diona wanted was to make me appear foolish, clumsy and naïve in front of Rock simply to make herself look better.

Diona pushed Kim aside and slid her arms around Rock's neck, gazing longingly into his eyes. "You and I were meant to be married, Rock. We understand each other. We've spent a lot of wonderful nights in each other's arms." Her lips formed the perfect Mona Lisa smile. "You know there's nothing I won't do for you."

He gently, but firmly disentangled her limbs from his neck and stepped back, silently putting distance between them as he shook his head. "I don't know you at all."

Diona cut Zelda a sidewise glance.

Zelda scooted to the edge of the sofa, her face flushed with agitation. "Dear boy, what's holding you back? See here, she's the proper match for you in every way and I wholeheartedly approve of her. Once you marry and produce a grandchild, I'll revise my will and die a happy woman. What more do you need?"

His face became a stony mask. "No one betrays me and gets a second chance. It's over, Diona. Go home to your father, the only person you'd do anything for."

Diona ignored the stinging accusation in his advice and fell against him, her hands gripping his collar. "Listen to your mother, Rock," she said in a tearful voice, obviously desperate to melt his heart. "She only wants what's best for us and that's why she approves of our marriage. We don't need to have a large wedding, at least not now. We could take the midnight flight to Las Vegas, say our vows tonight and start working on a family right away. Rock, I love you!" A large tear slid down her cheek. "I want to have your child!"

His eyes narrowed as he pried her crushing fingers from the collar of his expensive suit. "Leave, Diona. That's all I have to say."

"You'll regret this," Diona spat and jerked her hands away from his. "One day you're going to realize that you've lost the love of your life, but by that time I'll be happily married to someone else; someone richer and more handsome than you!" She picked up Kim's crystal candy dish on the coffee table and hurled it into the fireplace, shattering it. "I hate you!" With that, she charged out of the room.

"Rock! Don't be a fool. Go after her!" Zelda bellowed.

"Bravo," Kim countered in a bored tone and clapped her hands as Diona stomped out of sight. "The white queen shows her true colors." However when she glanced at Rock, his lack of emotion startled her.

Suddenly, the ugly truth became like an elephant in the room.

She spun around, facing him. "You knew about her disguise all along, didn't you?"

His brows furrowed and he suddenly began rubbing the back of his neck. "Look...Kim, I can explain..."

Her mouth gaped. How could she have been so naïve, so blind? "You used me, didn't you?" she cried as her heart began to break. "All you wanted was to make her jealous to pay her back for what she did to you. I can see that now."

Rock placed his wide palms on Kim's shoulders, gripping them tight. "That's not true, darling. I swear it. I simply wanted to keep her away from me and presenting you as my wife was the only way I could think of to force her to keep her distance."

She pushed him away. "Don't insult my intelligence, Rock. You could have cleared the air immediately." She pointed in the direction of Diona's exit. "You *should* have settled things with her the moment she showed up looking like she'd just come off her shift at the psych ward. You didn't need to set up this little drama. No, you wanted to pit us against each other."

Somewhere at the far end of the hallway, more glass broke as a door slammed.

He shook his head. "Honestly, I didn't mean for that to happen, Kim. I thought that if I went along with their ruse, Mother would eventually see Diona for the deceiver she is and admit that she shouldn't have tried to interfere in my life."

Did he really believe he could extract an apology from Zelda, much less her cooperation?

"Get away from me, Rock. It's over; your little game played itself out and now it's time for me to get back to what I was doing before you knocked on my door with champagne and a trumped-up story."

Before she could walk away, he took her hands in his and held them tightly. "Don't go." He looked intently into her eyes as Zelda silently watched. "Please, Kim, stay. I don't love Diona and I know now that if I'd forgiven her and married her anyway, it wouldn't have lasted long because she *never* made me feel the way you do." He pulled her close. "It's you, Kim. You're the one who makes my pulse fly off the charts. You're the one I think about all the time when we're not together. You're the one I want to serve coffee in bed for the rest of my life. And you know why? Because I'm falling in love with *you*."

She backed away. "No, no, I can't listen to this. It's not true. You told me how you feel about someone using you for your own gain, so why would you do it to me if you really cared about me? I don't want to end up just like my mother. She fell for every good-looking guy with a wallet full of money and a fast line, and we both know what happened to her."

YEOW!!

Sharp claws gouged the back of Kim's leg. She gasped and stumbled backward to get her heel off Roscoe's paw, almost falling over him. "Ouch! Rock—"

Luckily, Rock's long arms reached out and caught her before she fell, but in doing so, he almost tripped as Sasha dashed out from under the couch and tore after Roscoe. The monstrous tabby raced across the living room with a fat Chihuahua yipping at his tail, his barrel-like stomach getting in the way every time he tried to slip under a piece of furniture.

"Stop it! Stop it!" Zelda cried. "Rock, do something about that mean little dog! It's going to hurt Roscoe!"

"She's not mean," Kim snapped, wiping a thin line of blood trickling from her calf. "She's just trying to protect me."

Roscoe scrambled under the tree and began to climb the branches as Sasha circled the balsam fir, barking shrilly.

"No! No! Not my beautiful tree!" Kim screamed. "Rock, get him out of there before he tears it all to—"

Roscoe had nearly reached the blinking star when the Christmas tree began to topple. Ornaments and jingling bells flew off and bounced across the carpet as the barrel-shaped kitty meowed and furiously fought to untangle himself from being stuck between two branches. It might as well have been a building coming down for all the noise it made.

Rock and Kim ran to the tree to find the buried cat. Zelda sprang from her place on the sofa, crunching on ornaments as she rushed toward the tree and knelt on the floor, calling loudly to Roscoe. She pulled him from the jangled mess and held him to her chest, even though he meowed and squirmed to get away.

"Roscoe, Roscoe, oh, my darling! I'm so happy you're all right," she exclaimed as she clutched him and rose to her feet. "My poor, sweet pussy cat—" Her voice abruptly cut off midway through the last word, as though something had startled her.

"Oh-h-h-h," she said, clutching her chest, her face turning ashen. Roscoe meowed and sprung away from her, landing on the floor with a loud thud. "Buggers..."

Then the mighty Zelda Henderson collapsed.

Chapter 10

Tuesday, late afternoon, December 22

The television blared in Zelda's hospital room as Kim stood outside the doorway, mulling over what to say to her. She'd come to check on Rock's mother and to politely, but firmly, tell Zelda what she thought of the woman's hair-brained scheme to reunite her son with his former Jezebel of a girlfriend, but for some unaccountable reason, the words weren't easy to come by. Deep down, Kim regretted upsetting Zelda just before she collapsed and truly wished for Zelda to make a full recovery—then go back to sunny St. Petersburg and stay there.

A doctor emerged from the patient room across the hallway, giving her a curious look. She turned away and took a deep breath, knowing she couldn't hesitate forever.

"Hello, Zelda," she said as she held her uneasiness in check and stepped through the doorway. "How are you feeling?"

Zelda seemed genuinely surprised to see her, but offered a grateful smile. She appeared restless and uncomfortable in her light green, standard issue hospital gown. Her short, white hair needed combing and dark circles under her eyes formed shadows on her pale face.

"Hello, dear, come over here and sit down." She removed a pair of red-framed eyeglasses and placed them on her bed tray. "It's good to see a familiar face for a change. I'm doing well enough, but the situation will definitely improve once my son arrives to take me home. The doctor says it was a bit of indigestion that caused all the pain,

114

though it certainly felt like more than tummy trouble to me."

She shook her head. "I thought I was having a heart attack! Alas, I shan't be eating anchovy pizza again." She picked up the remote and turned off the television. "How is Roscoe coming along? Is he being fed at the proper time?"

Kim nodded and slipped off her down-filled, floor-length coat as she perched on the edge of a cold, hard chair. If Rock was due to show up soon, she didn't want to stay long. "Roscoe is just fine. I checked on him this morning before I left for the hospital and he was sprawled across the sofa, watching the lights on the Christmas tree."

"Oh, dear." Zelda clasped her hands together. "The tree, is it salvageable? If I recall, it fell over."

Yeah, it went down all right, with your pot-bellied cat clinging to the top like King Kong...

Kim cleared her throat. "The tree looks great. There are just a few crooked branches that we can easily straighten. I went back to Rock's place this morning after he'd left for work and cleaned up the mess. I had to vacuum about a dozen crushed bulbs out of the carpet, but miraculously, the crystal icicles survived." She shrugged. "It had too many ornaments on it, anyway."

Zelda ran a hand through her mussed hair. "I don't remember anything, but my son tells me that when I collapsed, you took charge of me, calling 911 and accompanying us in the ambulance to the hospital."

"Why, yes, of course," Kim said, surprised. "I couldn't leave you, Zelda. I had to make sure you would be properly taken care of."

Zelda reached out and clasped Kim's hand. "My dear, I owe you a debt of gratitude. I've been wrong about you, stubbornly so. You've been good to me ever since we met, despite the way I've treated you."

Kim sprung from her chair and stood close to the bed. "Zelda, I'm the one who needs to apologize. I should never have said the things I did about your smoking and pretending to be ill," she said, blurting out the words before she realized she had spoken them. "Those issues are between you and Rock and I had no place commenting on them. You have every right to want to see your son happily married, regardless of which path you choose to deal with him, and I don't blame you for trying."

"Nonsense, my dear," Zelda countered. "It was wrong to interfere in his life. My son is a brilliant businessman, but in the past he has made some irrational decisions concerning women. I simply want him to be happy and thought I was doing the right thing by encouraging the match between him and Diona."

Zelda expelled a sigh of regret. "Diona came to me a couple weeks ago, literally crying on my shoulder that Rock had broken her heart over a misunderstanding. She's quite an actress, that one. At any rate, she convinced me to help her get into Rock's flat to confront him again, promising that if he took her back and married her, she'd settle him down and start a family."

In a crystal-clear moment, Kim suddenly saw Zelda in a new light and clearly understood the lonely old woman's plight. She patted Zelda's hand. "You want a grandchild to fill that empty spot inside you..."

Zelda's eyes misted. "Yes, I do," she said, her voice heavy with longing. "I want a little girl to take the place of the one I never had. A darling little princess that I can dress up and spoil at will. Is that so terrible?"

"Not at all," Kim managed to reply as she blinked back a sympathetic tear. Zelda simply needed someone to shower with her love.

"I'm not getting any younger, you know, and neither of my sons possess the slightest attraction whatsoever to marriage. At least Rock is interested in women, but Patrick is so focused on racing that fool car of his, sometimes I wonder if he isn't a bit..." Zelda finished the sentence with a wave of her hand and another loud sigh. "Enough of that," she said briskly, returning to her former spunkiness. "It's pointless to dwell on such things. My sons will marry when they are ready and I must accept that." She glanced downward then looked up with a hopeful expression. "I see you're still wearing the wedding rings."

Kim held up her hand. The magnificent four-carat diamond sparkled despite the dimness of the lights on the walls above Zelda's bed. "I moved back into my own place last night, and I haven't had a chance to give the set back to Rock yet, so this is the safest place to keep it."

"He is truly in love with you, you know."

Kim froze, embarrassed by Zelda's abrupt assertion. "I realize that's what you want to believe, but it isn't true. He's simply infatuated with me."

Zelda pursed her lips, her face reflecting the stern, imperious attitude she usually reserved for Rock. "My dear, I know my son and I've never seen him so happy in his life. His eyes shine brighter than the star on top of your tree when you come into the room. The signs were subtle at first, but the more time you two spent together, the more obvious it became." She paused for a moment, her face softening. "Of course, I didn't want to believe it. I hate to admit when I'm wrong, and although you come from a respectable family, you didn't have either the present social standing or connections that Diona had, so I dismissed his growing affection for you as mere infatuation."

"Hold it right there, Zelda." Kim held up her hand like a school monitor directing traffic. "Just so you know...as far as the bedroom is concerned, I've never participated in anything more intimate than a handshake with your son. We shared the same bed, but he spent the night on his side and I on mine."

Zelda burst out with an astonished laugh. "My son would never agree to such a thing."

"Oh, yes, he would," Kim fired back matter-of-factly, "if the stakes were high enough and those were the only terms he could get."

"I see. What are those terms, pray tell?"

Kim briefly explained the circumstances that led to her agreement with Rock and the rules they set.

"You're *perfect* for him." Zelda laughed in delight. "Don't you see?" Color began to return to her face as her eyes flashed with their former brilliance. "You're hard-working, trustworthy, compassionate toward others and you're a wonderful cook—everything he needs in a wife and the mother of his children."

"Whoa," Kim said and backed away with her hands up. "Zelda, you're jumping to a lot of conclusions. I understand you want to find the perfect wife for your son, but I am definitely not his type and he's *absolutely* not mine. We had an interesting four days together. That's all it was. Before last Friday, we barely knew each other. I'll admit it was fun getting to know him after I laid down a few rules, but I'm not in the same league as the women I've seen him with at parties in the complex. I'm not tall, willowy or elegant, radiating sexuality like expensive perfume. I'm exactly what you described, hardworking and down to earth—too predictable for a man who lives on the edge. That's why Rock convinced me to be his stand-in wife. He knew he could count on me to smile and play the part—while he was secretly pitting me against *her*. He never meant it to turn into anything more and, frankly, neither did I. Now he's gone back to his normal routine, and I'm...I'm..."

I'm what? Going back to my cracker box condo and my clinging dog? Showing up at the hospital next week and acting as though nothing ever happened?

A deep sadness fell upon her shoulders like a heavy blanket of gloom. Everything she'd just pointed out about her brief relationship with Rock was true. Their closeness was idyllic while it lasted, but it wasn't real.

Zelda didn't seem to think so. She looked gravely disappointed as she said, "But my dear, he told you that he loved you. What more do you need? If you're looking for my permission, I would be honored to have you as my daughter-in-law."

"Falling in love in just four days?" Kim shook her head. "He simply got swept into the moment. We both did..."

Emotions welling inside her signaled to Kim that she needed to leave. It made no sense to dwell on "what might have been" any longer, even if Zelda did just give her wholehearted blessing.

She slipped into the satiny sleeves of her silvery pink coat and snatched her purse off the floor. "I'd better be on my way."

She reached into her coat pocket and pulled out her cell phone, checking the time. "I'm meeting a friend for dinner, but if I don't get going, I'm going to be late." Kim held out her hand. "I'm glad you're back to normal and ready to be discharged. Have a safe trip to Vail. Merry Christmas, Zelda."

Zelda clasped Kim's hands tightly as her eyes glistened. "A very merry Christmas to you, too, my dear."

Kim gently pulled away and walked to the door.

"Just one more thing," Zelda called out in an urgent tone.

Kim stopped and, with a silent sigh, looked past her shoulder.

"I deeply apologize for startling you last night by making certain information public about past issues with your family, and especially your father. I had no idea that you weren't aware of his identity."

"That's all right," Kim replied softly. "I realize that you didn't mean to hurt me. As you said, you were simply trying to protect your son."

"Do you want the information my investigator gathered? I can have it delivered to you by tomorrow."

Kim thought for a moment then turned toward her. "Thank you

for your concern, Zelda, but I believe I need more time. I've spent my entire life wondering who he was, whether I resembled him at all and wishing I could meet him. You'd think I would consider it a dream come true to finally get the opportunity to contact him, but it was such a shock when you revealed the information, I wasn't prepared. I need more time to decide on my next step and if I do obtain the investigator's report, to prepare myself for possible rejection. After all, even if I choose to contact him, there's no guarantee he'll acknowledge me much less accept me with open arms. I've been around for thirty-four years. At any time he could have contacted me, but he never did."

Zelda nodded. "I understand. However, if you change your mind, you only need to ask and the information is yours. You only live once. Please don't give up on him. *Or my son.*"

Kim said goodbye and left.

As she rode the elevator down to the parking garage, Kim wondered if she'd ever meet the right man—a man she could trust. A man she could love without reservation.

"Well, I'm not going to sit around and wait for Prince Charming to fall out of the sky," she said to herself, her voice echoing in the empty elevator car. "I'm going to do what Kate Middleton did when her prince left her high and dry. Going to dig out my address book and start partying!"

Chapter 11

Wednesday, late morning, December 23

Kim sat curled up on the sofa with a mug of eggnog-flavored coffee and her first new year's resolution, a brand new day planner that she intended to fill with activities.

Sasha lay quietly by her side, watching her.

"The first thing I'm going to do is join a fitness club," she said to Sasha and penciled in a note to ask her friend, Candy, in 303E for referrals. Then she made an additional note to ask Candy to lunch. "That's a great place to meet people, especially healthy ones." She picked up her reindeer mug and stared at the empty spot where the tree used to sit. "No way am I hanging out with any guys who drink, smoke and watch reruns of Duck Dynasty. I want a guy who's sophisticated, successful, likes to travel and understands the art of romance..."

Rock's face suddenly flashed through her mind and her heart took a nosedive off the pier of heartbreak bay.

She cleared her throat. "Okay, back to the task at hand." Setting down her coffee, she bent over her book.

"January 1st, shopping for new clothes," she announced as she began to pencil in her resolutions. "January 2nd, go on a diet to get into those new clothes. January 3rd, join a fitness club to get a great-looking shape and meet new friends so I have new places to wear said clothes." She tapped Sasha on the nose with the eraser end of the pencil. "Absolutely no blind dates. Candy is always trying to set me up, but I need to meet the guy first." She stared into the fire. "Hmmm...maybe I should grow my hair long—"

Her cell phone rang. Kim picked it up and saw Rock's name in the display. Her heart rate jumped into overdrive as she stared at the letters. Her first impulse was to let it ring, but her hand acted of its own accord and pressed the green button.

"Hello..."

"Merry Christmas, Kim," Rock's deep voice said in a cheerful tone. "Are you busy right now?"

Yes, I'm busy planning you out of my life...

"I'm in the middle of something. Why?"

"I'm leaving for Vail in a couple hours and I thought you'd like to have your Christmas tree back for the holidays. I won't be back in town until Sunday night."

She still had his elevator card so she could slip into his place and take it down by herself after he'd left, but he probably didn't want her coming into his residence without him there.

That's why he's asking you to come and get it now, ditz-brain...

Though she thought it best not to see him again, she knew it would take several hours to dismantle the tree and pack up all of the ornaments, not to mention the rest of the holiday decorations she'd used to decorate his place, minus the crystal candy dish that Diona made the object of her tantrum, of course.

She sighed. "I suppose I could drop what I'm doing and come up to your place. I need to give you back the rings, anyway."

"Great," he said sounding a little too happy for her liking. Perhaps he was relieved to cleanse his life of all reminders of her and everything that had happened. "See you in five."

"Ten," she corrected. "I have to get dressed."

He hesitated for a moment. "Ten it is. See you then."

Kim tossed the phone on the sofa and took off for the bedroom with Sasha following on her heels. She had less than ten minutes to dress, fix her hair and put on cosmetics. Eight minutes later, she picked up her phone and headed for the door, wearing red jeans and a white turtleneck sweater. In record time, she'd moussed her hair, applied moisturizer and makeup and adorned her ears with Christmas bells.

"You be a good girl now," she said to Sasha as she finished her preparations with a shot of perfume on her way out the door. "No, you have to stay here, but I'm coming back in a little while with the Christmas tree. We're going to make some hot chocolate and have a decorating party!"

She didn't take the time to think about what she was doing until she'd stepped into Rock's private elevator, slipped the key card in the slot and watched the doors silently close on her. The mirrors lining the car made it impossible not to notice her appearance—and make a few adjustments.

Why am I so worried about how I look? I'm just going up there to get the darn tree! No chit chat, no dinging around, just throw the stuff in boxes and get the heck out of Dodge.

Suddenly the doors whispered open. Willie Nelson's "Frosty the Snowman" echoed through the foyer as Rock stood in the entryway holding two tankards of steaming liquid, wearing that same silly Santa hat that he'd worn the night he asked her to be his make-believe wife. He wore a pair of snug-fitting jeans and a collared red sweater that zippered up the front, left open at the neck.

"Merry Christmas, darling." He held out a tankard. "Have some hot cider. I'm celebrating. Mother is in Vail by now at my brother's house so I have a few hours of blessed peace before I have to join them. The best part is that she's on his case now about getting married instead of mine."

Kim warily accepted the mug. "Look, I'm just here to take down the tree. I-I don't have time to party. I have to get back to Sasha. She's all alone at my place."

Rock smiled handsomely as he gazed into her eyes. "No problem. I'll help you with it. Cheers." He held up his tankard as he entwined his free hand around hers. "I'll walk you to the living room."

Her stomach fluttered at his touch, but she kept her cool, doing her best to keep her nervousness at bay as they walked along the hallway, sipping their cider. When they reached the living room, Kim found a fire glowing in the hearth, the flames reflecting off the ornaments on the tree like tiny scarlet and gold lights. Rock pulled off his Santa hat and tossed it under the tree. Then he took her tankard and set it on the coffee table, along with his, and pulled her close.

"Rock, I can't—"

Before she could finish he surrounded her with his arms, his mouth covering hers with a deep, passionate kiss. Her palms pressed against his chest at first, but the gentle strength of his embrace melded her to his body. His heartbeat pounded under her fingertips, rivaling the thundering speed of her own. She took in the scent of his spicy cologne and her resolve began to melt.

Okay, just one kiss—to say goodbye...

The rich, soothing voice of Karen Carpenter suddenly filled the room as she sang, "Have Yourself a Merry Little Christmas."

"I can't have a merry Christmas without you," Rock murmured into her ear and began to slow dance with her around the living room. "I need you Kim. The last two nights have been miserable without you."

"This is a bad idea," Kim said in a shaking voice as her chin rested against his arm. "I knew I shouldn't have come here."

"Yeah, but I'm very glad you did," he confessed. "This place hasn't been the same since you left."

124

"Looks the same to me," Kim said as she leaned into his arms, moving in perfect time to the music.

"It's too quiet and empty here without you. I'm empty without you."

She pulled away as a familiar panic welled inside her. "I—I should go."

Instead of grasping her hands in his, he released her. "If you want to leave, I'll understand. My housekeeper can dismantle the tree and bring it down to you when she comes back to work next week, but I'm asking you to please...stay. You belong here with me," he said in a husky voice. "I'm in love with you, Kim and that's all there is to it."

She looked up at him. "Do you realize what you're saying? You've only known me as a friend for five days."

He smiled and squeezed her fingers. "Six, but who's counting. I've come to know more about you in the time we've been together than I learned about Diona in ten months."

Kim laughed wryly. "Except that you've never had sex with me."

"You're right," he said seriously, his dark-eyed gaze pinning hers. "This is the first time in my life I've ever fallen in love with the person first, instead of her body and you know what—I've come to realize that's why all of my relationships eventually fizzle out. At the end of the day, there needs to be more."

She shook her head. "Rock, this is crazy. What guarantee do I have that things will work out between us?"

He gently cupped her face with his hands. "You don't. That's life; but you'll never have a shot at happiness if you're not willing at least to try. Listen," he said in earnest, "I know what's driving your fear. You're worried I'm going to leave you and break your heart, but love is a two-way street. What's to prevent you from breaking mine?"

"Rock, I would never do that."

125

"Well, neither would I. When Diona betrayed me, I didn't know if I could ever trust another woman again, but I should never have trusted her in the first place." He lifted her ring hand to his lips and kissed her fingers. "You're different and you've made me realize what I've been missing all along." He slid his arms around her again and looked deeply into her eyes. "Give me a chance, Kim. That's all I'm asking."

Her solitaire sparkled in the firelight.

"What about the rings?" She removed the jewelry and dropped it in his hand. "It's a beautiful set, but you probably should return it now that we don't need it any longer."

Rock went down on one knee. "Kim, will you marry me? Not today, not tomorrow, but when the time is right. You decide. There's no hurry. Until then, we'll take it one day at a time."

Tears began to pool in her eyes. "Rock, I can't believe you're—"

He smiled and brushed a tear from her cheek. "Hey, I'll even throw in my Artisan mixer. What do you say?"

All she could do was laugh with happiness as she wiped her eyes.

He disconnected the set and slipped the engagement ring back on her finger then stood up again and guided her to the sofa. They sat quietly together in front of the fire, listening to Bing Crosby sing "White Christmas."

Rock slid his arm around her and pulled her close. "How would you like to spend Christmas with my family in Vail? You and The Sausage could fly up there with me this evening."

Kim frowned. "Isn't this a tad late to be trying to get a plane ticket?"

Rock laughed aloud. "Baby, the way we're going, you don't need a ticket. I've chartered a private jet. When we arrive in Vail, a limousine will meet us at the airport to take us to my brother, Patrick's place.

He's got one of those big chalets built into the side of a mountain."

"I'd love to."

"We'll make it a surprise. Mother will be overjoyed to see you. And Patrick," Rock added with a wry smile, "will be relieved that her attention has shifted to someone else."

Wow, Kim thought in amazement and remembered what Zelda said about wanting her as a daughter-in-law. It all happened so fast— engaged to Rock, accepted into his family.

I'm living Veronica's dream...

Though she didn't mention it, she knew the happiness her presence would bring Zelda—not to mention the solid prospect of possible future grandchildren!

Rock's BlackBerry began to ring. He reached over and picked it off the coffee table. "That's odd. It's Al Grabowski. He never calls unless there's a problem."

"Hello, Al," he said into the speakerphone. "What's up?"

"Say, I just wanted to let you know that the executive board met this mornin' to discuss the bylaws vote about pets in the buildin'."

Kim stared at Rock, nervously wondering why they'd called a special session. Could it be that they'd learned about her deal with Rock to get his vote?

Rock squeezed her hand and stared at the phone. "What happened?"

"Turns out, they suspended the vote indefinitely and instead agreed to hire a consultant to study the problem."

Kim and Rock stared at each other for a moment then burst out laughing.

"Is something wrong, Mr. Henderson?"

"Not at all, Al. Thanks for letting me know. Merry Christmas!"

"Yah, sure," Al said, sounding bewildered. "Merry Christmas to you and Miss Kim, too."

Rock ended the call and turned to Kim, sliding his arms around her. "Things always work out for the best, don't they? Merry Christmas, darling."

The End

Thank you for purchasing this book. If you enjoyed it, please feel free to leave me a review at www.Amazon.com/dp/B00IOWTC28

Thank you from the bottom of my heart. I look forward to sharing more stories with you in this series.

About the Author

Denise Devine has had a passion for books since the second grade when she discovered Little House on the Prairie by Laura Ingalls Wilder. She wrote her first book, a mystery, at age thirteen and has been writing ever since. She lives on six wooded acres in East Bethel, Minnesota with her husband, Steve and her three problem (feline) children, Mocha, Lambchop and Tigger. She's presently a cat person, but she loves all animals and they often find their way into her books. Besides reading and writing, Denise also loves to study and travel.

For more information, please visit her at:

Website: www.deniseannettedevine.com

Facebook: www.facebook.com/deniseannettedevine

Pinterest: www.Pinterest.com/denisedevine1

Other Works by the Author

This Time Forever

Romance and Mystery Under the Northern Lights

Hot Shot

Coming Soon!

Happy New Year, Baby

Counting Your Blessings Series
Book 2